CW00847487

THE TIME DRIVER

G. A. FRANKS

For all the children I have worked with, who have taught me so much.

CHASE

Chase Connors is 13 years old and is a funny, caring, and smart sort of boy, who is lucky enough to be blessed with the kind of cherubic looks that little old grannies can't help but stop and fawn over in the street. He doesn't like going to school, and isn't keen on most subjects, except for science, which he loves, and technology, which he also loves, but not quite as much as science. Chase's hobby is horology, which means that he is interested in anything to do with time, especially finding and fixing old wristwatches, of which he has a large collection that he enjoys very much.

But...

For all his many good qualities, Chase is also the type of person who makes what teachers like to call "poor choices". In fact, he regularly makes the kind of choices that some people might call "a bit silly" or "a tad thoughtless" ...or maybe even "outright terrible".

Chase is particularly lucky, because he lives in a lovely little town called Bisby by the Sea. He lives there with his dad, Jon (who is a musician) and his dad's partner, Max (who is a car fanatic and a sort of doctor that helps people talk about their feelings).

BISBY BY THE SEA

B isby by the Sea is a very interesting and beautiful place to live. All the houses are painted in wild and wonderful colours and the harbour is always full of fishing boats with names like "Evergreen" that come and go all day and bob up and down all night. Everywhere in Bisby smells of seaside and waffles and fish and chips, and the narrow, cobbled streets are like a maze, only with lots of hills and tunnels and hidden places to explore.

Bisby by the Sea is also an interesting place to live in the winter, when the tourists have all gone home. That's when ice-cold waves smash into the rocks and mysterious fog rolls in from the sea, blanketing the whole of Bisby Bay in a thick, soupy mist. A small island called Clod sits off Bisby's coast and you can take a boat trip there if the sea is calm. Clod has many secrets of its own, including a ruined castle and some old smugglers' caves. Bisby by the Sea really is the perfect place to live.

But...

It is also a very strange place indeed. A very strange place filled with some very interesting people, where all sorts of unusual things happen.

As you will soon see.

PART I

PROLOGUE

"I'm afraid you've left me no choice but to exclude you from the school permanently."

The headmistress' words felt like a hammer blow slamming straight into Chase's stomach. He could tell from her sour expression, and the fact that his father had been called in and was sitting beside him with a face like thunder, that she really meant business this time.

"I'm sorry, Chase, I truly am." Harriet Hatchett rested her pointy elbows on her vast oak desk and sighed. "But sadly, this is the end for you here at Bisby Secondary School. There are only so many times I can stick my neck out to save you, no matter how much you may excel in certain subjects. I've had numerous parents complain about the appalling way you've treated their children; some have even withdrawn them from the school because of you, and quite frankly, a fifth explosion in the science lab is five times too many. Poor Mr White lost a substantial amount of hair and both eyebrows this time."

Chase gulped. Surely this wasn't happening – he'd been in trouble loads of times, and usually just ended up writing an apology and maybe missing lunchtime for a few days. But excluded... for ever? This was bad, extremely bad. "But... but Mr White is almost bald anyway," he blurted out without thinking.

His father slapped a hand down on the desk and a loud *crack* echoed around the room. "That's *enough*, young man!" Chase was stunned; he had never seen his father so cross. "I happen to know that Mr White is only bald because of your *last* unauthorised so-called 'science experiment'. Poor old Neville, I've known him for years, long before he was a teacher. He's a changed man, you know, he gave up playing the drums because he was so afraid of bangs. Imagine that – a drummer scared of bangs! And all because of *my* son! Do you have any idea how embarrassing that is for me? You've put me in a right spot here."

"It wasn't even that big of an explosion this time!" protested Chase.

"Exactly!" barked Mrs Hatchett. "What if next time I'm phoning parents to let them know that their child has been seriously hurt because a pupil decided to try and create nitro-glycerine instead of a saline solution... again? Imagine the consequences!"

Chase had no answer. Thinking about consequences was something that his brain didn't do. He was only curious to find out if he *could* do things, not if he *should* do things.

Then the worst part happened.

Worse than the explosion.

Or the previous four explosions... and that melting thing that one time.

Even worse than the moment when Mr White had discovered his eyebrows were missing. And even worse than the imminent expulsion.

A single tear ran down his father's cheek.

He had never known his father to cry, not once. His dad would always talk through his emotions, or he'd find ways to express them, (mainly by playing his guitar very loud). But crying was new, and it left Chase with a deeply unpleasant hollow sensation in his stomach.

"Luckily," said Mrs Hatchett, sounding somewhat calmer, "I've managed to pull some strings for you. A new headmaster has recently taken over that other secondary school on the edge of town, the one they finished building last year, the 'Academy for Raising Standards in Exceptionalism'. He's one of these..." She paused and her nose wrinkled up, as if she had smelt something unpleasant. "Fancy, *modern* headmasters. He's supposed to be the bee's knees. Has friends in high places apparently, he went straight in at the top, never taught a day in his life, the lucky so and so. It's some new government strategy – now they're saying if you've run a business then you can run a school, even if you can't teach. 'A new breed of super-heads', they call them and there's some competition to find the best one. It's an insult if you ask me. Anyway, new academy pupils are supposed to pass an entry exam, all terribly strict and whatnot. They only want the crème de la crème at the Academy for Raising Standards in Exceptionalism apparently. Nothing at all to do with a million-pound competition prize, I'm sure," she huffed.

Chase's father looked blank. "I see, but what does this have to do with Chase, may I ask?"

"Well, luckily for you, it so happens that Barbera, the school admissions lady for the county, and I go way back. She owes me a favour or two, so I managed to persuade her to slip Chase on to the academy's entry list for me as a special case.

Consider it my parting gift to you both. This is a rare opportunity, Chase. A real chance at a fresh start, in a school many students would give their right arm to attend. Don't waste it, my boy, don't... waste... it... Chase? Are you listening to me?"

Chase wasn't listening. His eyes had glazed over, and he was utterly distracted by a decidedly scruffy-looking owl sitting in a tree outside the head's window that seemed for all the world as if it was staring right back at him. "Sorry, right, thanks yes," he muttered. "New school."

1

THE ACADEMY

"**B**rand-new school, same old boring assembly."

Chase's eyes wandered around his new school hall while the deputy head banged on about something boring. The hall was much fancier than the one at Bisby secondary, but at the end of the day, was still an extremely dull place to be. 'Yup,' he thought. 'No question about it – assembly equals boring, every time.' Thankfully, he considered himself somewhat of an expert at assembly-survival techniques, which was mostly a matter of looking around and trying to work out who would get squashed if one of the light fittings were to fall. It was good for a few minutes of entertainment and was marginally more interesting than counting ceiling tiles.

Once the assembly had finally finished, Chase was shuffled off to a very beige room, for a very beige welcome meeting with an older student, who was wearing a badge that proudly proclaimed: 'Richard Pritchard, student representative – here to help.' It didn't take long for Chase to discover that in actuality, 'Richard Pritchard, student representative', was profoundly dull and not-at-all happy to help as he banged on endlessly about how important the student reps were and how essential they were for the smooth day-to-day running of the school.

"What happened to the old headmaster?" asked Chase finally, managing to seize upon a brief gap between some boring rule about something-or-other and some other boring rule about some other something-or-other.

The question caught Pritchard off guard and his eyebrows shot up like a pair of furry caterpillars making a bid for freedom from the world's most boring face. "What? Why would you ask that? Who cares what happened to him?"

"Well," Chase adopted his well-practised "innocent" face, "this school is super-new and, if it's so great, why would the first headmaster leave so soon after it opened?"

Pritchard puffed out his chest, clearly proud of his terribly important 'insider knowledge', and lowered his voice to a grating adenoidal whisper: "You remember the *incident* last summer?"

Chase certainly did remember – who could forget? The previous summer there had been a bonkers couple of days when the whole town's old plumbing had gone crazy, and the vintage Ferris wheel on the seafront had broken loose and wiped out half the high street. Strangely, though, the events of that night were rarely mentioned among the citizens of Bisby, who had a curious tendency to quickly shrug off such unusual occurrences, what with them being so common in the little town.

Pritchard continued: "Well, they say that the next morning, the old headmaster turned up in the staff room here ranting and raving about a monster in his bathroom. Pretty soon after that, he recommended Mr Thorne for the job and handed in his notice – luckily for us. Headmaster Thorne is an incredible leader, and we are all blessed to have him. Anyway Connors, let's get you to your first lesson, maths with Mr Mould."

2

WELL, THAT'S NOT RIGHT

Mr Mould the maths teacher turned out to be a towering, humourless brute of a man. As he slid into his seat and unpacked his pencil case, Chase couldn't help but stare up at the human tank as he flopped a crisp, fresh new maths book on to the desk. He was built like a bodybuilder, with rippling muscles that sought to burst out of the bland shirt constraining them. A huge, bushy moustache squatted above Mould's top lip, extending for several inches out from either side of his face, before curling down to the ground, giving him the appearance of having a perpetual frown. Chase's mind was already working overtime coming up with mean names for him. Mocking the teachers was fair game for the pupils in any school and a brutal roasting of the maths teacher would be a sure-fire way to make a few friends at break time. *Speaking of which...* He raised a hand: "Excuse me, Sir, what time's break?" The soft scribbling of pencils all around Chase stopped as though someone had flicked a switch.

Mould paused mid-step, his gigantic shoe hovering just above the ground for what seemed like an eternity. "I don't know how you did things at that second-rate hole you call Bisby Secondary, Mr Connors," he growled. "But here at the Academy for Raising Standards in Exceptionalism, pupils do not speak unless spoken to."

"But I put my hand up, Sir!" Chase protested.

"AND I DID NOT INVITE YOU TO SPEAK! A RAISED HAND ALONE DOES NOT WARRANT PERMISSION TO SPEAK DURING A LESSON." With remarkable speed, Mould brought his massive head down to Chase's eye level, shoving it so close that he could spot the tiny crumbs of digestive biscuit trapped in the man-mountain's mighty moustache. "I can see you're going to be one to watch, Mr Connors," he snarled. "*Special case* or not. You're not special in my room, boy, not by a long shot. In fact, I see nothing special about you at all! Consider your card marked, lad, well and truly marked. Pansy, write him up." He gesticulated to a gold-badge-wearing student with a huge shock of bright red hair, who duly produced a small notebook from her blazer pocket and frantically scribbled in it without breaking her sneering gaze.

Mould slowly and deliberately unfolded himself back to his full height, his massive arms folded across his chest. "And as for your question – it's time when it's time, boy." With that, he turned on his heels, returned to the front of the class and lowered himself into a chair that gave a timid *creak* in protest. "Pages 25 to 100, calculus and algebra, begin."

Chase slowly exhaled; he hadn't even realised he had been holding his breath. Being afraid of teachers wasn't something he was used to, but he had to admit that 'Baldy Mouldy' had put the wind up him - not a good start! He thought about his dad and Max, they'd been so devastated when he'd been excluded from BSS and so thrilled at the second chance he'd been given to go to the academy. If he blew it in the first week, they'd be heartbroken, not to mention the fact that he'd be grounded for life – or worse. *'No,' he thought. 'Not this time, I'm not going to let them down again.'*

Then he opened the maths book and another thought occurred to him: *'Wait a minute. Pages 25 to 100? That's 75 pages of maths in a single lesson!'* His hand was already in motion to ask if he had heard correctly when he managed to intercept it with his other hand and wrestle it back under the desk. *'No!'* He decided not to aggravate the teacher anymore and just make a start and see how far he got. Maybe it was so many pages because the work was really simple, or the writing was really big or something.

He looked at the first question. It was *not* in big writing – and it was *not* simple. Trying to stay calm, but starting to panic a bit, he checked the next question... and the next... and the next... Each was longer and more complicated than the one before... and that was only the first five pages – there were 70 more after that!

He glanced at his watch; for luck, he'd chosen to wear his current favourite from his collection. It was a gold divers'-style watch with chunky hands, a shiny blue face and a wide bezel that glowed in the dark and could be used at depths of up to 50 metres. He'd washed both his dad's and his partner Max's cars every week for three months to afford it, but it was well worth it. Not that washing Max's car was ever a chore – he had a sleek silver sports car from the 1980s, with cool gull-wing doors that attracted attention wherever it went, even if it was a little slow! But it was still somewhat of a stark contrast to Dad's rusty old gig-wagon.

The watch's luminous hands pointed to 10.08. This was a good sign – at his last school, morning break had been at 10.30, so break time here couldn't be much later than that, surely? A quick glance around revealed that everyone else was face-down in their books, their pencils furiously scrabbling back and forth. Not one person was looking around, or counting on their fingers, or making a spit ball, or using a set square as a ninja star, or goofing off in any way at all.

A heavy fog descended over Chase's thoughts. He'd felt it when he first entered the classroom and had written it off as nerves, but it was getting worse with each passing second. It wasn't a headache as such, it was more like his brain was full of a thick, syrupy goo that weighed it down and made every thought heavy and slow. *'It's probably just stuffy in here,'* he decided and, with the hope of a snack and some fresh air not being too far away, tried his best to push the fog aside, turned his attention to the workbook and got stuck into question one.

It took an age. An agonising, super-difficult age, but eventually he found an answer and, as a reward to himself, he peeked at his watch again. The luminous hands indicated the time was 10.09. *'Well, that's not right.'* He risked a glance at the clock above Mould's big, bald head. It also read 10.09. He shook his hand to bring some feeling back to his numb fingers, rubbed his eyes, blinked, and checked again.

10.09.

Both timepieces still read 10.09. He considered whispering across to another kid to check, but the nearest was the red-haired student rep with the golden badge who'd already written him up, so that was a no-go. *'Must just be a weird coincidence, both must have stopped at nine minutes past 10,'* he decided finally, experiencing more than a little irritation at the fact that the battery was running out in his favourite watch. But at least there was a silver lining, in that any excuse to take the back off a watch and fiddle about with the insides was fine by him. Resolving to get through the day without any further trouble, he turned back to the book and pressed on – it would be break time at any moment, he was sure.

The questions plodded by, each more taxing than the last. Determined not to keep checking his watch, he managed to grind his way through six more, before curiosity finally got the better of him and he decided to check the time again.

10.10.

'What? That's odd, the battery can't be flat, then, maybe it's running slow, really, slow.' He checked the clock on the wall – it, too, read 10.10. He looked down at his book – six questions done. "Huh," he murmured to himself. "Imagine if I really could do that much in one minute."

"What was that Connors?"

Mould was already out of his seat and making his way across the room. Chase winced; he'd spoken out loud without realising it. "Nothing, Sir, I, my watch has broken, that's all, Sir."

Mould was drawing closer, but something was... off. Chase watched in fascination as the brute lumbered towards him in slow motion. His desk was only a few metres away, and yet the journey appeared to be taking him several minutes. The strangest thing about the bizarre scene was that he didn't *appear* to be moving slowly he just... wasn't getting anywhere and yet appeared utterly oblivious to the fact. It reminded Chase of when a video game character gets stuck on scenery and keeps walking on the spot. He risked a glance around, not one person had looked up from their work. No... not quite. Tucked away at the back of the room was someone he hadn't spotted before – a pale girl with jet-black hair, who was staring straight at him with a stricken expression on her face.

Mould still hadn't crossed the short distance between them, although his face had changed colour quite significantly in the time it had taken Chase to look around. Now his forehead had turned deep maroon, and a ball of spittle was forming on his lips. The whole weird experience was starting to make Chase feel quite unwell. His mouth filled with saliva and tiny coloured dots danced in front of his eyes as he looked up at the clock again.

Any keen horologist will tell you that they can always spot a clock's hand when it moves, even from a distance. It's like they have a radar for it. And any *really* keen horologist will tell you that, if something is not quite right with the way that a clock is working, they will know simply by watching how its hands move. To some horologists, the way that a timepiece moves its hands is as telling as when a doctor takes your temperature or measures your pulse, and to Chase, it was clear that something was very wrong. The hands on both the wall clock and his own watch were – he struggled to find the right word – they were... *straining!* The irregular movement was infinitesimally small. But it was definitely there. It was as though the hands were pushing against something or maybe being held back by some unseen force. He checked his favourite watch again, mired in confusion, and starting to feel extremely nauseous indeed. Mould's reflection loomed in its deep-blue face, as the minute hand finally managed to fight its way on to the 11th minute.

As a general rule, neither clocks nor watches are typically in the habit of making *bonging* noises on the 11th minute. On the hour, sure, clocks love *bonging* on the hour. Some will even play a whole tune in celebration, and they love it so much that they'll treat you to a little preview every 15 minutes. But on the 11th minute, *bongs* aren't a thing, which is why Chase was so shocked when he heard his watch, which didn't *bong* anyway, make a loud *thud* sound as the minute hand finally defeated whatever unseen force had been holding it back and it slid into place at 10.11.

"ENOUGH! I will not suffer this level of disruption in my lessons! That is strike two – Pansy note that down." Mould gesticulated at the red-haired girl, who was already scribbling in her little book again.

Chase's every instinct was screaming at him to punch the great oaf and run out of this awful school for ever. But even as his clenched knuckles paled; his father's disappointed face flashed through his mind accompanied by another wave of nausea, and, instead of lashing out, all he could manage was a feeble, "Sorry Sir," before turning back to the never-ending maths task. It was 10.11. Still.

3

DELYTH

It stayed 10.11 for what felt like hours, then 10.12 for days. It seemed to take weeks to reach 10.13 and by the time 10.29 finally came around, Chase was convinced he'd been in that one maths lesson for longer than he'd been alive up to that point.

At 10.30, all the other pupils abruptly stood up in unison. No bell had sounded, nor had there been any sort of signal from the teacher but, acting as one, the students silently collected their bags and headed off down the corridor with none of the clatter and clamour that one usually finds at the end of a lesson.

Chase hesitated for a moment, torn between an overwhelming desire to get out of the room as quickly as possible and the temptation to speak to Mould and try to explain that he hadn't meant to cause a problem, but the dark-haired girl made up his mind for him. She was marching along with all the other students but kept sneaking glances back over her shoulder at him, as though she was hoping he would follow her. His mind made up, he slung his bag over his shoulder and set off before he lost sight of her.

"Hey," he sidled up behind the girl as the crowd dispersed. "Do I know you? You look familiar." She glared back at him for a moment, her jaw tightly clenched. Then, without a word, she turned on her heels and stomped off through the nearest door. Undeterred, Chase followed her, and they emerged into a leafy courtyard where small groups of students stood huddled together. "Hey!" he called after her, "today's my first day, I..."

"I know it's your first day!" She spat the words with such venom that it stopped him in his tracks. "I can't believe you don't remember me! And what's worse is that I never thought I'd be glad to see *you* of all people! But here we are and, unbelievably, I'm relieved to see you... Even if *you* are the last person I expected to see *here*."

"Thanks, I think," Chase said with a lopsided grin. "But you don't *seem* very happy, to be honest." The girl sighed and rolled her eyes. "Delyth... Delyth Maddocks."

Chase blinked. "What is?"

She took a step towards him, putting her face close to his, "I AM!" she half-whispered, half-shouted. "*I'm* Delyth Maddocks, me! My name is Delyth Maddocks... Oh my... You really don't remember me, do you?"

Over the course of Chase's 13-and-a-bit years, he had made a great many mistakes, more than a few enemies, and hardly any casual acquaintances. This meant that he had a very long list of handy excuses and a very short list of people whose names he cared to remember. He thought about explaining this to Delyth for a moment, but instead he decided to fall back on a good, old-fashioned lie. "*Ooooh!*" He threw a palm to his forehead in feigned frustration. "Delyth, of course, now I..."

"Just don't, Connors."

Chase also had enough experience with lying to know

when it was worth it and when it wasn't, and the tone of Delyth's voice made it abundantly clear that this was one of those times when it wasn't.

"We don't have time," she said. "Meet me by the old pier tonight at seven and I'll explain everything."

"What do you mean we don't have time?" asked Chase. "Break only started like a minute ago."

"Precisely."

Three short, sharp *beeps* rang out over the courtyard and the students began filing back inside.

"What *is* going on here?" Chase looked down at his watch, it read 10.50. "It can't be 10.50 already. That wasn't 20 minutes, it was closer to 20 seconds!"

Delyth was already heading back into the school. "Meet me at the entrance to the old pier later – and you'd better hurry up now. Don't be late to class, the headmaster hates lateness – it's an instant detention."

4

I WASN'T LURKING

C hase was deeply relieved to find that the next lesson was his favourite – science. Feeling somewhat befuddled by his unusual morning, and far more tired than he was used to before 11 o'clock in the morning, he took a moment to look around the laboratory. It was pretty much like the ones in his old school – there were long tables, white coats and goggles, and locked cabinets full of weird and wonderful devices waiting to be fiddled with. The main difference was that, unlike Bisby Secondary, everything was gleaming and new and well-cared-for and appeared not to have come from the last century. Some of the students from his maths class were here too, annoyingly, the redhead student rep Abigail Pansy was present, but there was no sign of Delyth. Out of habit, he made sure to check the clock on the wall, it read 10.51, the same as his own watch. Reassured by this, he searched for an empty chair and vowed at least to try to impress.

"Do I know you?" sneered the teacher, making a show of wrinkling her nose as she looked Chase up and down. She had a distinctly unfriendly face and an expression that made her look as if she'd swallowed a wasp.

"No, Miss, today's my first day, I'm Chase Connors, sent over from BSS."

"Ah yes," she plonked a book on the table. "The *special case* – I remember the memo now. I am Miss Harries, now hurry up and take a seat and let's get started. Students, turn to page 75 and read chapter 16, then answer the questions you find at the end. Once you have completed the questions, I would like an essay of at least three pages on the principles of quantum mechanics. Off you go, get on with it."

For the first time since arriving at the academy, Chase felt a flicker of happiness. Quantum mechanics was something that fascinated him, but it was a long way from the more basic subjects they had covered at his old school. In fact, he was convinced it wasn't on the secondary science curriculum at all – but he wasn't going to complain as it might be a handy opportunity to show off his love of the subject and all things related to time and space.

He opened the book and set about grinding his way through the chapter, it was much harder going than he had expected, but determination to prove himself to his dad drove him on.

Then a bad thing happened.

It began as a quiet gurgle deep down in his bowels.

Then a sort of "falling" sensation inside.

Then a sharp pain in his stomach as his mouth filled with saliva.

"Miss," he began, raising his hand, "please may I be excused?"

The teacher shot him a surprised glance. "Absolutely not, Connors."

"But Miss," he squeaked, "I really need the loo. I think I'm going to throw up!" Chase was painfully aware of the fact that every other student in the room was staring right at him, and (albeit rather more dimly) also aware of the fact that it was somehow apparently only 10.52 according to the class clock. Neither of which were his primary concerns when a resounding *gurgle* erupted from his stomach loud enough to make everyone look up from their texts as the bitter sting of bile reached his throat. He clutched a hand over his mouth desperately trying to hold in the contents of his stomach as they tried to escape. Seeing his eyes widen, Miss Harries gave a peculiar smile, as though she was taking cruel pleasure in his discomfort. "Go," she snapped. "Now! And don't be long."

Feeling somewhat worse for wear, having ejected everything he had eaten in the past 24 hours, Chase wobbled back up the corridor with his head spinning and his stomach hurting. He was about to turn the handle on his classroom door when something caught his attention: The wall displays – there were none. There was only a long corridor with blank white walls. He would have expected them to have been filled with work and achievements and information like every other school in the world, but there was nothing at all. The more he thought about it, the more he realised that he hadn't seen displays anywhere in the whole school. No English, no chemistry or biology, physics or drama, no poems, no art, no trips or productions, PE or RE or PHSCE or ICT or DT or MFL or any other acronyms. There wasn't even any of the students' work. It was just blank wall after blank wall.

"What are you doing hanging around in the corridor? I've been looking for you." The redhead student rep Abigail Pansy came stamping towards him like an angry bull, clutching her ever-present notepad. She brandished her pen under Chase's nose. "That's it, '*Special case Chase*', you're for it now. Report to the headmaster's office."

"What for?" Chase could feel his blood starting to boil. "I asked permission to go to the toilet."

"You were given permission to visit the toilet, *not* hang around lurking in the corridor. Miss Harries specifically said, 'Don't be long,' and you *were* long – too long." She scribbled something in her pad and snapped it shut with a flourish.

The pain in Chase's stomach gave way to boiling rage. "It's my first day! Come on, give me a break. I wasn't 'lurking', I was having a look at the... walls, I guess."

"Head's office now! Don't make it even worse for yourself." Before he could protest any further, Pansy took Chase by the arm and frogmarched him off.

5

THE HEADMASTER

S itting outside the headmaster's office, waiting for the inevitable telling-off, Chase couldn't quite believe he'd already ended up in trouble. It wasn't even the first time this week! He'd only been thrown out of BSS two days earlier so this was a new record, even for him.

When the headmaster's door finally opened, the man who emerged was tall and thin, with leathery skin that looked too big for his slight frame. His jet-black eyes glistened like lumps of coal and wispy tails of grey hair dangled down from behind each of his ears. The faint hint of what might once have been a beard clung to his chin, forming a thorny garden of uneven patches of black and grey bristles.

"You've had quite the first day, Connors." The head's accent took Chase by surprise, he sounded almost local, but not exactly; it was a strange mix, almost *exotic*. "I don't believe I've ever had a student brought before me for so many transgressions in a single day before, let alone on their first day, before lunch no less. My disappointment is displaced only by disbelief." The man stalked back into his office and Chase silently followed him. "Sit," he commanded.

The headmaster slid into a wing-backed chair behind a large oak desk, not unlike Mrs Hatchett's one back in BSS. Chase idly wondered if all headteachers had the same desk, perhaps ordered from www.intimidatingdesksforboostingheadmastersegos.com. A brass sign perched on the desktop read: 'Angus Thorne – Headmaster.'

Chase couldn't help but notice that, aside from an unusually large and dramatic painting of what appeared to be a heavily bearded 18th-century pirate in front of a sailing ship, the desk and chair were the only old-fashioned items in the room. Well, maybe apart from the smell, which was oaky and sweet with a hint of ozone and mustiness that reminded him of the charity shops in town – it somehow smelt old. But everything else was as clean, crisp, and new as the rest of the academy. Glass shelves, lit from beneath, emerged from the walls, each displaying an interesting oddity of some type or another. Chase, however, had become instantly obsessed with the most unexpected and striking feature of Thorne's office – the clocks – there were dozens of them. There had to be at least 20, all identical and plain white with no numbers. They were neatly arranged on the same wall, each telling a different time and each with a small, blank panel underneath that served no apparent purpose.

"Do you have anything to offer by way of explanation for your behaviour?"

Chase jumped at the question; he'd been so engrossed in staring at the clocks, he'd almost forgotten why he was here. He gave it some thought for a moment, which was not as easy as it should have been. Under normal circumstances, snappy comebacks were a bit of a speciality of his, but this time his usual snarky repartee was failing him, a couple of factors were making it rather difficult to be on top teacher-teasing form.

Firstly, his stomach was really hurting – it felt as though someone had swapped out his guts for a washing machine on a spin cycle. And secondly, it was freezing cold in the head's office, despite it being a pleasant June day outside. The headmaster's words turned to mist in the air, lingering for a moment longer than they should – the whole experience was deeply unsettling.

"Wub! Wubbwubwub! Wub wub wub wub wubbub wub?" The head's voice sounded far away, like he was speaking down a toilet-roll tube.

Chase's knees turned to jelly, and he sought out the safety of a clock. It always helped him when things were a bit *off*. It gave his mind something else to think about, imagining all the mechanisms behind the face perfectly slotting together in a symphony of synchronicity. He focussed on the wall of clocks, only to find that the sight of all those hands *ticking* and *tocking* out of sync with each other made him feel even worse than before. He had no idea what Thorne had said to him. All he could think about was getting out of the freezing cold room and into the relative safety of the nearest toilet. "Sir, I'm sorry about today," he mumbled. "I didn't know all the rules and I'm not feeling well at all, Sir – my tummy hurts, and I feel dizzy."

A predatory smile spread across Thorne's face. It was the type of smile one might imagine a spider giving to an unfortunate fly that has made an impromptu visit to its web. "If you are to remain here, then I strongly advise you to familiarise yourself with the rules and to improve your constitution as a matter of urgency. There is no time for the weak in mind or body here at the Academy for Raising Standards in Exceptionalism. You will have an after-school detention for one hour, whereupon you will complete a series of lines stating that you will modify your behaviour and maintain the standards of excellence demanded by the academy. This will be communicated to your father by my secretary and is neither transferrable nor negotiable. Failure to attend will result in your immediate and permanent exclusion. Do you understand, Master Connors?"

Chase was stunned. He understood all right, but that didn't make him any less angry. An after-school detention! On his first day! For basically nothing! Quietly fuming, he nodded, being sure to keep his mouth clamped firmly shut and his expression as neutral as he could manage.

"Off you go, Connors. I shall see you back here at 3.15pm. Do not let our paths cross in this manner again."

6

DETENTION

When 3.15 finally arrived, Chase felt as though he had been at school for a week already, rather than just one particularly long and rubbish day. After his run-in with the head, things hadn't improved at all. Lunch had proven to be a traumatic affair where he had choked down an amorphous, grey blob of something that he presumed was supposed to be mash, accompanied by an unidentifiable slop that most closely resembled a puddle of cat vomit. Even the puddings had been inedible – he'd rejected the so-called 'jelly' on sight. He knew full well what jelly looked like, and the murky, greasy slime presented to him had looked far more like something a plumber might find in a U-bend than food. Instead, he'd settled on a 'rock cake' that, as far as he could tell, had been an actual *rock-cake* and he was sure he'd chipped a molar or two tackling it.

The final nail in the lunch coffin was that it felt as if the whole awful ordeal had been over in what had felt like 10 minutes at most. There had been no chance to enjoy the freedom from lessons at all. His favourite watch said otherwise, but said watch was clearly not having a good day, either. The hands were still twitching and jerking as though pushing against some unseen force, and the time it displayed never made sense. He'd hoped to catch up with Delyth again over the lunch break but hadn't managed to find her.

The final lesson had been English, which was never Chase's strong point, even on a good day, but today's lesson had reached previously undiscovered depths of horrible. The teacher had presented him with a text written in such old-fashioned writing that it may as well have been a foreign language. Then she'd expected him to identify and colour code instances of three forms of 'past participle, present and future perfect and future perfect continuous'.

Chase quite frankly had no clue what any of that meant, or how knowing it would ever conceivably benefit him in life, so after what felt like an hour – but the clock had insisted was 10 minutes – he had hit upon the idea of seeing if he could colour in a pretty pattern on the page with his highlighters that was subtle enough that the teacher wouldn't catch on to what he was up to.

Pleased to have had at least that one small victory in an otherwise hellish day, he looked at his watch – 3.16 on the dot, it was time to head back to Thorne's office for his detention.

Chase knocked on the door to the head's office. He waited a moment, but there was no answer, so he went to knock again...

His hand slowed to a crawl and a single breath slowly left his lips in a cloud of vapour. When his tensed knuckles finally met the door with a resounding *clonk,* he watched, fascinated, as the vibrations slowly travelled through his hand like ripples in a pond. *Clonk.* His next breath came, time picked up its pace and everything was back as it should be. The office door swung open, and a blast of freezing-cold air wafted out.

"Sit." Headmaster Thorne waved towards a table that had been set up beneath the wall of clocks. Atop it sat a single pen, a small glass of water, and a stack of lined paper at least a foot tall. "You will write down the following phrase until instructed to stop: '*I will cast off the shackles of my lackadaisical past and embrace the promise of a better future thanks to the Academy for Raising Standards in Exceptionalism.*'"

Chase winced – the fuzzy head he had felt in the office earlier had returned, and so had the pain in his stomach. "Do I have to write the school's whole name?" he asked. "Can't I shorten it?"

"No, you may not shorten it, Connors!" Thorne was visibly agitated, his eyes narrowed like a cobra about to strike. "You should find the equipment I have provided will be sufficient. If you require more paper, it will be supplied."

Chase didn't imagine he'd be needing more paper. He didn't expect to fill even a 10th of the hefty stack, or even a 100th – especially if his next trick worked. "Please Sir, who's that?" he asked, giving his most winning smile, and pointing at the large painting of the bearded pirate. "He looks bussin'. Is he a pirate?"

Teacher distraction was a skill he had honed over many years, and he considered himself quite the expert. Some teachers wouldn't bite once they'd grown wise to his methods. But others, with the right well-placed question, could be relied on to slip into a lengthy reminiscence or monologue before realising they had been duped and that time was running out for whatever task was at hand.

The headmaster fixed his cold gaze on Chase as though deciding which end of him to devour first. "That," hissed Thorne through gritted teeth, "is the late pirate captain and renowned adventurer Captain Fernando Víbora Van-Quish. He is not '*bussin*' – whatever that means! He is an ancestor of mine and worthy of your respect. Captain Van-Quish was a great man born of noble descent, son to a fearsome Germanic warrior-king and a Spanish princess said to be so beautiful that the earth and her seas and even the heavens themselves would shower her with gifts wherever she went. Men of sensitive disposition were said to die from a broken heart whenever she was near, such was the pain of witnessing her unattainable beauty."

"Wow!" Chase had intended to feign interest, but instead found himself unexpectedly intrigued by the story.

"Captain Van-Quish was blessed with a great power, a gift from the heavens given to him at birth to gain favour with his mother. He is rumoured to have been able to bend the minds and wills of those who trusted him, and that time itself dared not touch him for fear of his father and for love of his mother. If you were to believe the inscriptions in this frame, Captain Fernando Víbora Van-Quish was more than 300 years old when he sat for this painting."

Chase shivered; the room somehow felt even colder. "He looked good on it, Sir! What happened to him?"

Thorne ignored him. His eyes had glazed over as he stared into the middle distance. It gave Chase the creeps and an involuntary shudder ran through him as if someone had just walked over his grave.

"No one knows for sure," he announced finally, suddenly free of the strange trance. "Some say he was betrayed by someone close to him, that, although he could keep old age at bay, he was somewhat less murder-proof. Others say that he still walks this earth, seeking ways to fill his life with meaning after the loss of his one true love – a woman with skin as pale as snowfall, lips as red as blood and a sword so sharp that it could cut through a man's bones as easily as it cut through the air. And now, Chase Connors, enough of your feeble attempts at procrastination – *you will begin your full hour of writing.*"

A strange '*prickling*' sensation started inside Chase's head, as if he had suddenly developed pins and needles in his brain. Along with the odd prickling sensation came an extraordinary urge to get started on writing the lines, but as quickly as it had started, the odd sensation passed.

"Fortunately for you," continued Thorne, "I have a meeting to attend and will not be here to monitor you. However, if you attempt to leave early or even leave your seat, then I will be informed, and the consequences will be severe in the extreme."

With that, he grabbed a briefcase and swept out through a side door that Chase hadn't spotted before, a door with a brass plaque that read 'Headmaster's study'.

As soon as he was gone, Chase shook his head and scratched at his scalp, making sure nothing was crawling there. Then he checked to see how much time he had tricked Thorne into wasting. Much to his frustration, his watch displayed the exact same as when he had last looked at it – 3.16. It was as though no time at all had passed. "What is going on with this watch today?" he wondered aloud as the temperature plunged even further, and the pain in his stomach intensified. With a resigned sigh, he picked up the pen and began his first sentence.

'*I will cast off the shackles of my lackadaisical past and embrace the promise of a better future, thanks to the Academy for Raising Standards in Exceptionalism.*'

Again and again, he scribbled the lines, filling page after page after page, his head pounding and his pulse racing, and a faint buzzing sound tickling his eardrums.

'*I will cast off the shackles of my lackadaisical past and embrace the promise of a better future, thanks to the Academy for Raising Standards in Exceptionalism.*'

Over and over he took a fresh sheet and wrote down those despicable lines.

'*I will cast off the shackles of my lackadaisical past and embrace the promise of a better future, thanks to the Academy for Raising Standards in Exceptionalism.*'

By Chase's reckoning, it had been 20 head-thumping, gut-churning minutes since he started to write. He looked down at his treasured watch but, not for the first time that day, time itself had failed him and it took a moment for his brain to comprehend what he was seeing. At first glance, it appeared that the face of the watch was smeared with something greasy, perhaps some slime from the so-called jelly he had encountered in the lunch hall. Closer examination (and a quick wipe on his blazer sleeve) revealed that it was not greasy at all. It was out of focus.

His watch was out of focus with its own strap. Out of focus from everything else in the room – and humming. It had never hummed before.

He blinked, rubbed the corners of his eyes, and checked again. The entire face of the watch was blurred like a poorly tuned television screen, its hands fixed at 3.21. The massive pile of lines he'd written meant that there was no way he'd been working for only five minutes, so something odd was afoot – again. He was just pondering the fact that, having lived in Bisby all his life, oddness of some type or another was never far away, when he felt a sudden, unexpected respite from the bitter cold: A warmth was spreading up his arm. A warmth that was quickly turning into heat – the actually-getting-uncomfortable-very-quickly kind of heat. A heat that was coming from his wrist or, more specifically, his favourite wristwatch!

He peered at its blurred face closely... It wasn't out of focus at all – it was vibrating! Vibrating so fast that the entire watch was now barely visible at all. The faint hum coming from its mechanisms grew louder and shriller and the heat became unbearable, burning his skin. "Ow!" He leapt from his seat and tore the violently vibrating timepiece from his wrist, sending parts of the strap and buckle flying in all directions. He dropped it on the desk and examined his arm. Where the watch had been, his skin was red and blistered, smelt like burnt bacon and stung like crazy. Without stopping to think, he snatched the glass of water and poured it on to the bubbling flesh, managing to soak his pile of completed lines in the process. "No!" he shrieked, clutching his seared wrist. "Can this day get any worse?!"

Then the watch exploded.

Tiny cogs and wheels and pinions and springs flew into the air amidst a shower of glittering glass fragments. The mechanisms hurtled off into every corner of the room and a particularly large cog struck Chase straight between the eyes, slicing open a nasty cut and sending a stream of blood running down his nose and splattering over the soggy remains of all the work he had done so far.

Clutching at his bloodied face, he counted to five and tried to visualise his dad's face if he was excluded on the first day. Every bone in his body was screaming at him to smash up the stupid, freezing-cold office with its weird wall of clocks and its even weirder painting and run away to the beach and live for ever in one of the brightly coloured beach huts, living off a diet of fish and chips and candyfloss. It was a brilliant plan, apart from several glaringly obvious flaws, but the thought of it bought him the headspace he needed to calm down enough not to destroy the office.

With blood soaking his nose and his wrist still burning, he set off around the room on his hands and knees to recover as many parts of the destroyed watch as possible.

He was just crawling around behind Thorne's desk looking

for a missing pinion, when a strange thing caught his eye. A thin shaft of brilliant white light was visible between the standard-issue school carpet tiles and the skirting board at the base of the wall with the weird white clocks. There didn't appear to be any doorway in the wall, and yet there was clearly a room behind it, a very brightly lit room, at that.

Deciding that investigating further would be a bad idea, Chase leapt to his feet and shot a forlorn glance at the mushy mess on the table. Most of the paper was ruined by water, blood, or both. The wall of clocks offered no help as to how much time had passed, as each of the numberless timepieces showed a different time on its blank white face, and the small panels below each of the clocks were all equally as blank. There was no clue at all as to what their meaning could be, although he knew enough to speculate that they probably represented different cities in different time zones around the world. But precisely what a headmaster would need so many clocks for remained a mystery. Concluding that he'd had enough weirdness for one day, he resigned himself to having to knock on the door to the headmaster's study and enquire about the time and get some more paper and maybe even a plaster.

7

THE STUDY

C hase knocked on the door and waited a few seconds. There was no answer, so he knocked again. "Hello, is anyone in there?" he called out. "I've had a bit of an accident and I need some more paper please... and maybe a plaster, if you have one?" There was a faint rustling sound from behind the door and then, with a soft click, it popped open to reveal the room beyond.

The study was cramped and dark, its low ceiling and curved wooden walls making Chase feel as if he had somehow stepped into the bowels of an old sailing ship. A single candle flickered in a sconce and an ornate wooden desk occupied almost all the space.

Atop the desk squatted a tatty old owl whose keen yellow eyes followed Chase around the tiny room. "Hello? Is anyone here?" he asked, nervously keeping one eye on the strange bird, which he felt sure was supposed to be in a cage and not just free to wander about.

No reply came. The only sound he could hear was a faraway creaking, as though something was pressing against the walls from the outside. It was warm in the odd little room, too, much warmer than the bitter cold of Thorne's office. In fact, Chase realised that he was suddenly very hot, uncomfortably so. The room seemed to shift and blur around him and for a moment he thought he glimpsed a computer and a fireplace and a window, as if a collection of random memories and places had jumbled themselves together. The images faded and the walls of the study closed in around him, dark and cramped once more. Sweat beaded on his forehead and ran down his nose, mixing with his blood. His legs wobbled, and he clung to the edge of the desk as the room swayed beneath his feet. The owl cocked its head to one side as though curious about the unexpected intruder. Darkness formed around the edges of his vision and bile burned his throat. He closed his eyes and took a deep breath, willing the nausea to pass...

When he opened them, he was standing on the deck of a ship under a clear blue sky. Lights flashed all around him and it sounded as if a car alarm was going off somewhere. The sky turned black, and a huge churning hole appeared, threatening to consume him. Cold steel pressed against his neck...

He blinked and the ship was gone.

He was still in the creepy study with the creepy owl and blood and sweat caking his face, and a nasty hint of vomit in his mouth. "Ugh," he managed, swallowing a mouthful of saliva. "Hello? I need more paper please... hello? I think I'm not very well. Do you have any plasters or a bucket? I feel a bit sick."

No answer came, and he couldn't see how anyone could

possibly be hidden away in such a small space. Or, for that matter, how Thorne could have exited through it – but he had, and someone had to have let him in? "Hello," he called into the gloom again. "Where are you? Is anyone here?"

"Time to go," said a woman's voice.

8

AND NOW I'M HERE

The evening sun glittered off the waves, the last embers of its touch enough to tempt the keenest surfers to linger in the breakers. A warm breeze carried hints of fish and chips and the clatter of falling pennies in the arcades as it wafted past chattering families plodding their way up the hill from the beach. Chase knew every one of these sounds like the back of his hand – but what he didn't know was why he was hearing them.

"That looks nasty," said a voice. "What happened to you?"

The world around him slowly began to take form. The sources of the sounds and smells swam into place as he found himself sitting on a bench on the promenade. "Hey," said the voice, which he thought he recognised from somewhere – it was a girl's voice. "Are you OK? You look out of it."

He blinked a few times, drew a deep lungful of sea air, and pinched himself to make sure he wasn't dead or dreaming. He was neither. He was on a bench, on the promenade, close to the entrance of the newly built pier, on a lovely summer evening. A perfectly normal thing to be doing – except that a moment earlier he had been in a definitely-not-normal study. With an owl.

"I was on my way to meet you," said the voice. "I didn't think you'd show up, to be honest and why are you sitting here? I said the *old* pier."

Chase squinted up at the source of the voice. "Delyth!" He leapt to his feet. "What's going on? How did I get here?" She looked at him as if he had gone completely insane – which he thought he probably had. It wasn't entirely common for people to not know how they had got to places. At least, not until they are *really* old, anyway, like 40 – then it did seem quite common-place. "I was just in the headmaster's office doing a detention," he spluttered. "And now I'm here."

"Detention on your first day? Why am I not surprised?" She folded her arms and glared at him, her lower jaw jutting out in a show of disapproval. "Up to your old tricks already?"

"No." Chase was far beyond confused at this point. "I mean I was literally *just* in the head's office, like 10 seconds ago – and there was an owl! And my watch exploded, and I might have fainted, but... Now I'm here, with you, and I don't know how I got here or how you know me or what the heck is going on!"

Delyth glared at Chase for an uncomfortably long time, her bright green eyes boring into him like laser beams. "That's a lot to process," she announced finally. "But let's say – and I can't believe I'm saying this – but let's say for a moment that I believe you, maybe we should start again, from the beginning." She held out a hand. "Hi, I'm Delyth Maddocks, I was at BSS with you until my parents pulled me out and sent me to the academy because *some idiot* kept blowing up the science lab and stealing my lunch and calling me 'The Green-eyed Goblin'. Ring any bells?"

Chase swallowed hard; a warm flush spread up his cheeks.

It did ring a bell. A bell that he was unexpectedly very embarrassed about. "Oh! You! You look... different," he stammered. "I can't believe you had to change schools, because of me! That's..." He trailed off, his words failing him. It was one thing to have a chuckle at someone else's expense, but to be responsible for them having to change schools... Needles of shame poked at his insides. "I don't know what to say," he mumbled. "Sorry doesn't seem to cut it."

"It doesn't," she retorted. "But given the circumstances it'll have to do, so apology grudgingly accepted, but if you start any of that rubbish with me again, I swear I'll make your life a living hell. I'm not the same scared little girl as I was at BSS."

"I see that," Chase agreed with a smile. "Sorry I didn't recognise you; you look so different."

"I got contact lenses, grew up a bit and got a better haircut is all. You really are quite shallow, aren't you, Connors."

He had no comeback for that. It turned out that apparently he was.

"So anyway," continued Delyth. "Let's talk about the elephant in the room here. You and I both know that Bisby by the Sea can be a bit 'odd' at the best of times, I mean, all that business last summer for a start."

Chase nodded. "Yeah, my dad's band was playing at the Ship Inn that night. He swore blind there was a monster in the pub and then the plumbing went nuts and then *that* ran off!" He jabbed a finger towards the almost-finished new Ferris wheel.

"Right," said Delyth. "But now there's something super-weird going on at the Academy for Raising Standards in Exceptionalism."

"You can say that again," said Chase. "I mean, the name alone..."

"I don't mean the name!" she snapped. "I mean the weird

kids and the tummy pains and..." She stopped; her eyebrows furrowed. "There's the other thing, the big one, only I can't... it's... Nope, it's... it's gone again. I can't remember what the big, weird thing is again."

"Time," Chase finished for her. "Time is broken at the academy."

Delyth folded her arms went very quiet, clearly deep in thought. "You're right," she announced finally. "Thank heavens, I thought I was going bonkers! I noticed it straight away when I started there, but no one believed me and the longer I've been there, the harder it is to keep track and sometimes I just... forget. It's like time is so messed up that my brain can't process what's happening to me, so it shuts off. I was starting to think I was imagining it, like everyone says I am." Her cheeks darkened, "I was so glad to see you, even though you're horrible. I know you like science and clocks and time and all that stuff. I thought maybe *you'd* believe me."

Unsure how to respond, Chase dabbed at the cut on his forehead. "I do believe you," he said finally. "You're not imagining it, time's wrong there. I know it, I can 'see' it somehow, I've got proof." He fished the shattered remains of his favourite watch out of his pocket and held out the parts for her to examine. "Check this out, it blew up in detention."

She peered intently at the pile of broken bits, "And?"

"And watches don't just blow up, Delyth." He showed her his burnt wrist, "It went crazy, vibrating like it was pushing against something, like *time itself* was trying to force it backwards – *and* the headmaster has a wall of blank clocks in his room, which is plain weird. Something's up for sure, I think that's why you keep forgetting, I reckon that whatever he's up to plays tricks with your brain. Maybe the longer you're exposed to it, the harder it is to spot, like when the bath water goes cold when you've been in too long, but you don't feel it happening. Maybe that explains how I ended up here on the bench? Maybe Thorne messed with my mind, too?" He clasped his hands together and shuffled his feet around awkwardly for a moment. "Look, this is a bit embarrassing, and I'm sorry to ask, but... you said something about your tummy?"

Delyth's cheeks flushed an even darker shade. "When I first started at the academy, I kept getting an upset tummy and puking. It's not as bad now, but I still go home wanting to throw up sometimes."

"I had the same thing today," replied Chase. "My sickness got way worse when I went into the head's office, and my head felt crazy, too. I think whatever is breaking time and making us sick is probably in there somewhere." The sliver of light he had spotted under the clocks popped into his memory. "And I think I know where."

"There's something else weird," added Delyth. "When I first got to the academy, I hated the headmaster with a passion. He was so creepy, but now I keep catching myself thinking how great he is, and I've had literally *nothing* to do with him. If this was a movie, I'd swear I'd been brainwashed or something. The only thing keeping me from randomly wanting to worship at his feet is the fact that he reminds me of..." She stopped and turned away.

"Go on – please, Delyth."

She rounded on him. "You! He reminds me of *you*! There's something in the way he stalks around the school like he's better than everyone else. I've had enough of bullies to last me a lifetime, thanks to *you*. When I left BSS, I swore I'd never be pushed around ever again! So whatever weird tricks he's playing – he can count me *out*!"

"Ouch! Harsh, but fair, I guess," winced Chase. He was still trying to formulate a sincere-sounding apology when a loud burst of music came from his pocket. He pulled out his phone and glanced at the screen. "Ten missed messages and three missed calls! I'd better get home; I'll find you tomorrow at school. Send me a DM later, you can add me on SnapFace, my username is *Clockmaster42*. And for what it's worth, I am sorry, Delyth. I'll make it up to you, I promise. All of it, somehow."

9

GROUNDED

Chase knew he was in big trouble before he even got to the front door. His dad was in the driveway loading the car ready for a gig and the thunderous expression on his face was one Chase knew all too well.

"You're grounded." His dad didn't even wait for an excuse or explanation. "Detention on your first day in the only school still prepared to take you! You're lucky I'm playing a gig tonight or we'd be having a very long and unpleasant conversation right now. Max isn't back till late, but I've texted him what you've been up to, so don't go running to him for sympathy. Hand over your phone. I've already taken your computer and tablet and I've changed the Wi-Fi password and hidden the controllers for your console."

"But Dad, I need..."

"Phone! Now, hand it over. I'm sorry, son, but until you make amends, you're done. No internet for you at all, no computer, no consoles, no games, no Snapface, nothing. You can go to school, and you can do anything school-related that you need to, otherwise it's home and study for you." He slammed the boot shut on his battered old estate car and slid Chase's phone into his top pocket. "This is for your own good, son. You're so smart, you could do anything in this world, but if you waste this precious time, it gets a lot harder to make it back up later – trust me." He pointed at the cut on Chase's forehead, "Dare I ask what happened there?"

"Nothing, just got clumsy is all." Chase decided not to mention the fact that he had no clue if he'd even finished the detention at all and that his watch had blown up and he'd wound up on a bench with no idea how he'd got there – it didn't seem to be the right time.

Once his father had disappeared off down the road in a cloud of diesel smoke, Chase wandered up to his bedroom and opened the large wooden box containing his prized watch collection. He had about 20 to choose from. Unlike many other collectors, there was no real pattern or plan to his collection – he just picked up whatever caught his eye. There were old-fashioned pocket watches, fancy fake branded watches, diving watches, cheap novelty watches, retro watches, and a couple of particularly nice examples that he'd been given as gifts on special occasions.

After taking each one out, giving it a quick clean and checking it was telling the correct time, he took a moment to consider his options carefully – given what had happened in detention, there was a good chance that whichever watch he chose to wear next wouldn't survive the day. Whatever was causing time to misbehave at school had already destroyed his favourite, and he wasn't prepared to lose another. Faced with a tough decision, he closed his eyes and tried to visualise which of his collection he would be least bothered about losing if it came to it. A vivid image of his wrist bearing an odd choice popped into his mind and along with it came a flash of inspiration – he would pick out two different watches, one digital and one analogue, to see what would happen to them.

His choice for the digital was the one he had *imagined* himself wearing, a cheapo novelty effort called *RoboWatch* that he had won from a grabber machine in the arcade. Not the sort of thing he would normally be seen dead in at school, but in this case, it was worth the risk of being laughed at. (And, if he was honest, he did think it was cool in a quirky kind of way!) For the analogue he chose a *G-Wizz* branded watch that had probably been quite expensive in its day – but that day was at least two decades earlier. He'd never really bonded with it, so it was pretty much expendable, compared to his others. Pleased with his sacrificial choices, and the idea of taking two different types of watch to see how the school affected them, he fished out the remains of the wrecked dive watch from his pocket and spread them out on his sideboard. Several bits were missing, and some had been badly bent when it had blown up, it was a bin job for sure, nothing was even worth keeping for spares. With a sigh, he scooped up the parts and deposited them into the wastepaper basket. With that done, he reached for his phone to check if Delyth had messaged him yet, before remembering that there was no phone to grab – Dad had taken it, along with everything else worth doing.

In a foul mood, he went to bed early and fell into a fitful sleep, haunted by dreams of floating clocks, angry pirates, and flying cars.

When the morning sun finally peeped through his curtains, it was a decidedly bleary-eyed and grumpy Chase who dumbly nodded along through the inevitable breakfast lecture. He was well used to them by now, having been on the end of quite a few over the years, so he made sure to make all the correct grunts at all the correct times and give all the correct reassurances to get Dad and Max off his back.

With their warnings ringing in his ears, he made sure that both RoboWatch and the G-Wizz were firmly strapped to each wrist, tossed his rucksack over his shoulder, and headed off to the stupid academy with the stupid name and the stupid, creepy headmaster and his stupid freezing office with his stupid freaky owl and the *supremely* stupid watch-destroying broken time.

Morning registration was spent mostly holding his breath and waiting for the headmaster to arrive and grill him about escaping detention and leaving a soggy mess behind. But much to his surprise, nothing happened.

First lesson was double maths, and still no call to the head's office came – not that it was much better to be stuck in a 90-minute session that dragged along with all the pace of a sleepy snail out for a Sunday slither. He made sure to keep a close eye on both watches for any signs of time misbehaving, and it didn't take long.

The first clue was when by his (generally very good) reckoning, it should have been about two-thirds of the way through the agonising maths marathon, the wall clock still insisted it had only been 10 minutes since he had sat down. His acute sense of time, and the stabbing pains in his gut meant that knew full well that the school clock was telling a big fat lie.

The next clue that something nefarious was afoot, was

when one of the little digital bars on RoboWatch's face started to fade in and out, pulsing in a steady rhythm. He glanced around to see if anyone else was showing signs of noticing, but everyone else had their heads down, their noses deep in the improbably difficult calculations the teacher had demanded from them.

Baldy Mouldy was sat at his desk scribbling away at something or other, but every so often he would look up and glare around the room with an expression that suggested he was dying to catch someone out. His eyes lingered on Chase for an uncomfortably long while, and he could feel the man's gaze burning into the top of his head as he tried his best to appear as emotionless and robotic as the rest of the pupils – not an easy feat when his stomach was twisting itself into knots.

When break finally came around, Chase discreetly dashed for the same courtyard where he had met Delyth the day before. To his relief, she was there, seemingly waiting for him.

"Sent message, why no answer?" she demanded. "Use quick speak"

Chase quickly cottoned on to her plan, break only lasted for a minute or so at most, there was no chance for a normal conversation, it would have to be her so-called "quick speak". "Grounded – phone gone, pc gone, all gone." She winced in sympathy. Pleased she had understood, he rolled back his blazer sleeves and held up his wrists, proudly showing off the two watches. "Experiment!" he beamed.

As soon as she saw the brightly coloured RoboWatch, Delyth threw a hand over her mouth and attempted to stifle a laugh, but she wasn't quite quick enough and a loud snort came out of her nose instead. This immediately drew the attention of several pupils who scowled in their direction as though they had never heard laughter before, among them was dullard extraordinaire Richard Pritchard.

"Want see what happens," Chase said, grinning, ignoring the student rep as the three *beeps* sounded to announce the end of break. "I'll contact you somehow... Dad away week... His boyfriend Max is pushover... Leave with me."

"That's a strike, '*Special-Case Chase*' – and you, Maddocks!" announced a gleeful voice. Chase cursed under his breath, he hadn't spoken quickly enough, and Pritchard had managed to close the gap on them. "Dawdling and chatting when you should be moving swiftly on to the next lesson – a flagrant violation of academy policy. Keep this up, Connors, and you'll end up in detention twice in one week!"

Chase smiled weakly and winked at Delyth before striding off down the corridor, still ignoring Pritchard.

For the rest of the day, he kept a close eye on the classroom door, always expecting the headmaster's summons to come, but nothing happened. It was as though Thorne didn't care, or somehow didn't know, about his leaving the detention – which was a definite bonus. Deciding to put the whole bizarre situation out of his head, he dedicated his energy to keeping a careful eye on his two watches instead.

It was during an English lesson, that had already lasted for what felt like at least three hours, that the poor RoboWatch's display suddenly flickered for a moment before fading to black. The G-Wizz struggled through English too, its hands straining and twitching, until eventually they were vibrating so fast that they became an out-of-focus blur. When the lesson finally finished, he tried to spot if anyone else was wearing a watch. After all, he couldn't be the only person to have caught on to the broken time, but the stupid blazers everyone had to wear made it almost impossible to see.

By the time lunch break plodded around, Chase was barely

able to make it to the dining hall. His entire body ached; his eyeballs had given up trying to focus hours ago, his stomach had gone numb, and his brain felt like it wanted to ooze out of his ears. The sight of Delyth plopping down like a sack of spuds into the seat next to him managed to raise his spirits somewhat, if not his energy levels. "Well, I managed to get through the whole morning without throwing up and having to dash to the toilet again," he announced, shoving a mouthful of some odourless grey paste into his mouth. He presumed it was meant to be mashed potato, but it looked more like papier-mâché.

Delyth grimaced at the grey paste on her fork, "Yeah, that part gets better quite quickly, but I swear today has lasted like 10 hours already and we're only at lunchtime. How's your little robot friend getting along?"

Ignoring the sarcasm, Chase showed her the RoboWatch. "Dead."

Delyth frowned. "Is it? It doesn't look dead."

The digital display had flared back into life, the digits racing along at top speed. The pair watched it go for a few seconds until the LCD screen briefly exploded into multi-coloured swirls and turned dark once more with a quiet *pop*. "Well, I guess he's definitely dead now," she snickered. "I'm so sorry, it was a brave sacrifice. Had you and Robo been friends for long?"

Her sarcasm flew straight over Chase's head, he was engrossed in staring at the G-Wizz. He'd expected to see the now familiar straining as the hands appeared to push against some invisible force, but instead, the exact opposite was happening, and the hands were flying around the face much faster than they should be. "Huh," he whispered. "Look, it's going crazy. You know what, I bet it's because it's lunchtime!"

Delyth's jaw dropped open. "That's it! Thorne's got to be

slowing down time in lessons and speeding it up in break times somehow... but... but how!"

"And why?" added Chase.

The three beeps sounded, and lunch was over.

10

MERIDIAN

When Saturday morning rolled around, it took Chase quite some persuading, and a decent amount of pleading, but he eventually managed to badger Max to allow him to be 'ungrounded' long enough to wander into town to The Fancy Pasty so he could pick up an 'apology pasty' to make amends for the detention.

He was ambling along, enjoying the sea air, and pondering how Thorne could possibly be twisting time, when the hairs on the back of his neck suddenly crawled and prickled. He swatted at himself in a moment of panic, very much hoping not to find a large spider there. But there was nothing except a creeping sense that something was... *what?*

He looked around. Nothing was out place, except... him. *'Why did I come this way? I never come this way.'* He had walked into Bisby almost every day of his life and had never once taken this route until today. He always turned right at the weird shop that you only ever find by the seaside – the one that sells all sorts of random junk that people only ever buy on holiday. Stuff like novelty watches, outboard motors, overpriced hoodies, rubber seagulls, 30 types of fridge magnet, toothbrush holders made of driftwood and fake samurai swords. But today he had turned left and was now standing in a place that he couldn't remember having been to before – and it had an owl!

An interesting fact about life in Bisby by the Sea is that everybody knows everybody else, and everybody lives two lives. Their summertime life, when the tourists flock to the town in their thousands and the sun shines, and the money flows – and their wintertime life, when the sea turns grey, and the shutters come down on the gift shops and the stalls selling temporary tattoos and hair braids. This is the cycle of life in Bisby by the Sea. It is a place of beauty and mystery that has something for everyone...

But one thing that Chase was certain Bisby did *not* have – at any time of year – was great big owls that flew around in the daytime. Especially familiar-looking, tatty owls that land in the street right in front of you and glare up at you like an expectant child – which is precisely what was happening.

"You again!" He lunged for the bird, but it easily evaded him, leaping into the air and flitting down the street before deftly landing again. The erroneous avian twisted its head all the way around and stared straight back at Chase. It then performed a strange little dance and wandered off at a casual stroll, as though goading him to follow.

Charging off after it, Chase fully expected the bird to take flight once more and head to the skies, leaving him behind. But instead, it flapped its wings and ducked into the doorway of a shop which Chase was 100 per cent sure had never been there before.

He knew this because it was a clockmaker's shop. And Bisby did not have a clockmaker's shop...

Because if Bisby *did* have a clockmaker's shop, he would have known about it and been in there at every possible opportunity. Plus, this shop was weird. It wasn't some modern, faceless high-street store. It took only one look before you realised that this was exactly the mysterious sort of shop that a mysterious sort of owl would lead you to.

"What. The. Heck?" Chase stood rooted to the spot for several minutes staring at the run-down shop. It ticked all the boxes on the *"mysterious-shop-that's-popped-up-out-of-nowhere cliché checklist"*: Faded exterior and those old-fashioned leaded windows with circles in them that look all melty – *check*. A low, thatched roof that overhangs the door, casting a sinister shadow over the entrance – *check*. Weather-worn wattle and daub – *check*. General sense of foreboding – *check!*

Despite his poor decision-making skills and virtually non-existent self-control, Chase Connors was generally a far smarter-than-average sort of person, who instinctively understood that the appearance of a distinctly mysterious and conspicuously creepy old clockmaker's shop was almost certainly in some way associated with the time twisting weirdness taking place in the academy. It *had* to be – this was Bisby, after all!

He checked his watch; he'd worn a nondescript department-store job that he couldn't even remember how he'd ended up owning, it read 11.45am. If he claimed to Max that there had been a super-long queue at the 'Fancy Pasty' (which there inevitably would be anyway) then he almost certainly had time to pull off a little investigative work. It was worth the risk, he was already grounded, what else could they do – ground him more? Resolute, he examined the faded sign hanging over the entrance, it read 'Meridian' in a fancy sloping script.

With a deep breath and sweaty palms, he ventured into the

gloomy shadows and pushed the low door, which opened with a suitably mysterious *creeeak*.

He was barely through the door when his eyes nearly popped out of his head. The place was a horologist's heaven! Any thoughts of the owl he had chased inside were instantly forgotten as he gawked at the wondrous sights surrounding him. A sweet, musty smell greeted him, as though some exotic wood had recently been burning. The hairs on his arms and neck prickled and rose to attention – something about the air inside felt heavy and charged with ozone, the way it does before a thunderstorm.

The walls and low ceiling were covered in timepieces of every conceivable shape and sort, their gentle *ticks* and *tocks* playing a calming soundtrack at odds with the whirlwind of motion surrounding him. One wall had been entirely given over to intricately carved cuckoo clocks, each decorated with tiny figures that spun and danced and whirled around, blissfully happy in their equally tiny homes. Astronomical clocks were the theme on another wall, where golden suns and silver moons spiralled over, through and around each other, all framed against a painfully beautiful melding of supernovas and galaxies. Brightly coloured celestial bodies shared space with vines and creeping plants as they emerged from a wall painted a deep purple and speckled with minute golden stars.

In the centre of the cramped little shop, a single support pillar seemed to drip down from the ceiling, as though the wood had melted, or even that the shop had simply grown itself around what had once been a tree. The impressive column bore carvings that Chase knew to be the ancient Greek gods of time, Chronos, Aion, and Kairos. Each of them carried a totem with one hand and with the other, pointed to a bizarre clock, balanced on a needlepoint within a hollow inside the pillar, where three spinning silver orbs orbited around each other in a complex pattern.

"Do you like my shop?"

A small voice caught Chase unawares and his heart almost punched its way out of his chest. He had been so enthralled by the wonders surrounding him that he had somehow entirely missed the old lady waiting patiently behind a dusty old counter. She certainly made for a striking sight! A pair of half-moon spectacles perched on top of her bushy mane of black and grey hair, where they fought for space with an oversized red flower. One of her eyes was hidden behind a watchmaker's eyeglass, gazing into the back of a gold pocket watch, while the other was locked on to him. Even in her advanced years, there was a certain poise and elegance about the way she held herself that set his already frazzled nerves on edge. She looked more like royalty than a clockmaker.

"Hello." Chase forced a nervous smile. "This place is amazing!"

"Thank you, it's always nice to have a visitor," the old woman shut the pocket watch with a *click* and placed it on the counter. "I believe you may have missed my very best clock." She pointed a long, pale finger at his feet. "Look down."

A stunned gasp escaped Chase's lips. The entire floor of the tiny little shop was transparent! He was staring straight into a mass of spinning cogs and gears that appeared to go down for ever, plunging off into unseen depths, whirling and whirring beneath his feet. "Oh wow!" he exclaimed, struck with vertigo and exhilaration in equal measure. "That's beautiful! Is it done with mirrors?"

The old lady tittered. "Can't give away all my secrets now, can I? Not yet anyway."

Chase realised she had a hint of an accent; one he didn't

recognise. It sounded more like lots of different accents rolled into one, like an accent cocktail, or pasty...

'Pasty...Max.... Oh no!'

He'd been so focussed on the incredible shop full of clocks that he'd forgotten all about the actual *time*! "I'm so sorry," he backed towards the door. "I'm not supposed to be here, I've got to get going."

"Wait!" Something in the old lady's voice compelled Chase, and he froze on the spot. "That wristwatch you're wearing," she said. "May I see it, please?"

He hesitated, why would someone with a shop as wonderful as this be interested in the most boring watch on the planet? "Sure." He shrugged and rolled up his sleeve to show her the black plastic watch. "I'm a collector, I have some really nice pieces, but this is a rubbish one. My favourite is a..." He remembered that his favourite was now a pile of parts along with RoboWatch and the G-Wizz, which had finally melted itself to a halt during the last never-ending lesson the previous day. "Never mind, my favourite broke. Quite a few of my watches have broken recently as it goes."

"Well..." The old lady popped her eyepiece back in and gazed intently at the plastic cheapo special. "Isn't that a thing? Lots of broken watches you say? What an odd thing, I'd say you're not the first to have that happen, hmm?"

"Is that why you opened the shop? Have you been here long?" asked Chase, hedging his bets. He knew full well that the shop hadn't opened recently, there was more going on here than she was letting on, for sure. "Do lots of watches break in this town? Maybe... around the new school for instance?"

"Let me do you a little favour, collector to collector." She pulled out her eyepiece again and extended a hand, my name's Alejandra. Alejandra Rosamunda Vela, and you are?"

Chase shook her hand. "Chase Connors, pleased to meet you."

"Well Chase Connors, now that we are no longer strangers, I can tell you that I am most enamoured with this watch of yours. It's... unusual, like nothing else I have."

Chase looked around at the range of ornate and incredible timepieces surrounding them. "You can say that again! It's crap!"

"Crap to you perhaps, but there is something special about every timepiece, be it fantastical or mundane. Each and every clock has the power to contain the most unstoppable force known to man – time. Even this unassuming little watch of yours holds within it every moment that has ever been or will ever be. Every choice made and every hope and every regret. How often do you wish to turn back time, Chase Connors? Or wish it to hurry along? I've heard it said that every person on this earth wishes time away in one direction or another every single day that they are alive. It is a shared experience that transcends age, class, wealth, where you live, *when* you live, how you live and ultimately... when you no longer live at all. And even then, time only stops for your thoughts. For your body and those around you, it keeps on moving. You become a memory in time, and in time again you return to the universe, whose ongoing expansion is what gives us time in the first place. And all that power, all those possibilities and that unstoppable force are all *contained in here!*" She jabbed a finger towards Chase's watch. "In this tiny little plastic package attached to your wrist. Tell me, have you heard of Einstein, my boy?"

Chase was somewhat taken aback at how animated the elderly lady had become. She suddenly didn't seem so old, in fact, she even seemed to *look* younger. Her unexpected question pleased him, though – he knew all about Albert Einstein and his amazing theories to do with time. "Yes," he replied. "I've read a lot about his time-travel theories."

She appeared impressed with his answer. "Well, then you know that every clock is a tiny time machine. If you took that little plastic watch of yours to the top of a mountain, then you would find that it was infinitesimally faster than the same watch placed in the deepest cavern you could find."

"Yeah, they talked about that at my school, my old school I mean. It's pretty cool, but the ability to control time is..." He paused – he had been about to say that it was impossible, or only in films or TV. But there was more going on here than she was letting on, he knew it. "Impossible?" he ventured finally. "Wouldn't you say... scientifically speaking?"

The woman gave him an odd smile, "Is it, though? I mean, according to Einstein's rule, you could say that you do a little jump into the future every time you stand up! But science isn't the only amazing thing in this universe, Chase. Science is somewhat like the lens of this eyeglass. It lets us look closely at something, while the other eye is free to see a much bigger picture – a picture full of all sorts of things too big to fit into that little lens."

"What sort of things?" Chase was starting to feel as though they were sparring with each other.

The old woman gave him a knowing look, "Why don't you tell *me*, Chase Connors? What sorts of things have been breaking your watches? Are they scientific things, do you think... or are they something else?"

Chase thought for a moment, the entire situation seemed too bizarre to be real, but what *was* real was that Max was waiting for his lunch and time – no matter how amazing it might be – was running out for him to get home. "I really have to go, Mrs Vela," he announced. "You can keep the watch if you like, I honestly do have plenty of others."

"No no, that won't do, and please, call me Alejandra. No Chase, a trade must be made, always a trade. I have something very special to give you. Here, take this." She offered him her weathered hand. Clutched within it was the antique pocket watch she had been working on when he had first walked in. "I will accept no arguments, but make sure you use it and don't lock it away. Don't let its age fool you, sometimes old things are still capable of great things – age is only a number after all!"

Chase took the watch from her, carefully placed it into his jeans pocket and handed over his plastic cheapo special. Alejandra took it from him and appeared to be extremely pleased with the exchange. "Everything you need to know about that watch is written inside the casing, now hurry along, Chase Connors, don't get yourself in any more trouble than you already are! Not yet anyway. I'm sure I'll be seeing you soon."

Without realising quite how, Chase found himself ushered out of the shop and back into the unfamiliar street. It was only as the gulls sang their greedy songs and the warmth of the sun touched his cheeks that he realised that Alejandra hadn't answered his question about how long the shop had been there, and that she somehow seemed to know he was in trouble of some kind.

He took three steps and... *"The owl!"* He realised he'd completely forgotten all about the owl – she must have seen it. He glanced over his shoulder, half expecting the wonderful shop to have vanished into thin air. But it was still there, albeit with the door now firmly closed and adorned with a hand-written sign that read "Closed for lunch".

With a sigh, he dropped the watch into his pocket and, as with the owl, it somehow just... faded from his memory.

PART II

PART II

11

THE WATCH

The next week dragged along agonisingly slowly, each lesson seemingly lasting for hours, while breaktimes with Delyth flitted past in mere moments. The odious student reps were rarely far away and gleefully wrote Chase up several times for ridiculously minor infractions. Thankfully, he managed to avoid another run-in with Headmaster Thorne, who strangely never called him in about the whole detention fiasco.

He was pleased to discover that the ever-present sense of sickness and confusion lessened somewhat as the week went on, precisely as Delyth had promised it would. But an ever-expanding mountain of homework, rigorously completed under threat of having his grounding extended, meant that he didn't have much opportunity to ponder the time-warping conundrum that dogged his days.

He had almost completely forgotten about the mysterious shop and its enigmatic owner, until a particularly taxing double history lesson on the role of the turnip in the agricultural revolution blew out the last of his "not-actually-that-good, I-don't-mind-if-it-breaks" watches. He had spent what felt like hours watching the poor thing strain against time, its tiny cogs and gears fighting a valiant battle, but the effort was too much. When it finally came, the brave little watch's end had been spectacular, the glass face had cracked and imploded as though it had been under immense pressure, all three hands had melted down to stubs and Chase had once again come home from school with a burnt wrist, a broken watch, and an increasing sense of despair.

The loss of his last 'don't-care-that-much' watches came as something of a blow to Chase. He'd hoped to solve the 'mystery of broken time' without losing so much of his collection, but now he'd lost loads of watches and had solved approximately zero. The constantly shifting times at school and endless home-work tasks had worn him down so much that simply getting through each day took all the energy he could muster, the other pupils being so robotic all the time was starting to make sense.

That Thursday evening, as Chase stared glumly into his much-diminished watch collection, even the weather seemed to have caught his mood. A soupy sea mist had rolled in overnight and stubbornly hung over the beautiful town like a bad omen. The brightly painted houses lining the harbour vanished into the grey void and the usual to-ing and fro-ing of glass-bottom boats and fishing trips had all ground to a halt. Only the top of the still-under-construction Ferris wheel managed to pierce the silent veil of gloom over Bisby Bay. Teatime was at least an hour away and Dad was still on his *determined-to-knock-some-sense-into-you*' mission that had become his big deal ever since the whole debacle of being kicked out of BSS and then getting a detention on the first day at the academy.

Dumping his school uniform on the floor with a sigh and

searching around for something else to wear, he pondered simply giving up and not wearing a watch at all the next day, He'd proved his point – time itself was broken in the academy, and he strongly suspected that Headmaster Thorne, with his weird owl cupboard, freezing-cold office, spooky blank clocks, and freaky glowing skirting board was behind it all. But there was no way to prove it, Thorne had made sure of that.

He and Delyth had briefly talked about filming the time-bending effects on watches and the even weirder robotic students, but there was a *super*-strict ban on phones in the school. Bringing a phone into the academy was an instant exclusion, something neither he nor Delyth was willing to risk, especially with the ever-present student reps snooping around like Thorne's personal pack of bloodhounds.

The thought of Delyth made him instinctively reach into his jeans pocket for his phone – a habit he'd still not broken since Dad had confiscated it. Instead, his fingers closed around the cool metal of the pocket watch that Alejandra had insisted he take. The unexpected sensation gave him a jump. *"Of course, the watch! The shop – how did I forget?"*

He turned the old pocket watch over, running his fingertips across the fine filigree work that covered every inch of its golden case. Even in its somewhat dusty condition, it felt wonderful in his hands, like a smooth, golden pebble that had been rounded off by the sea. It had a pleasing weight to it, too – in fact, it was far heavier than any watch he'd ever come across before – and that was a lot of watches! Coldness radiated from within it, as though it had been stored in a freezer for a long time, and an unusual pulsing emanated from the casing like a tiny heartbeat, quite different from the usual 'tick tock' that clocks are known to be fond of. It was like nothing he had ever come across before, it felt somehow more *organic*.

A quick glance at his wall clock revealed that it was only

4.40pm, meaning there was plenty of time to investigate the strange pocket watch before tea and maybe even give it a good clean-up. He flipped its ornate latch back, and opened the casing...

...Hundreds of voices swirled around him, a choir chanting in unison, their words strange and unfamiliar and yet hauntingly beautiful at the same time. But as quickly as they had come, the voices faded away and his room faded with them. For a moment he was alone, lost in darkness, but then, eerie scenes – monochrome memories from his previous week swam out of the gloom and surrounded him, brought to life like scenes from a play, acted out by ghostly figures.

He saw himself in Thorne's office, clutching at his burnt wrist, and watched intrigued as the face of his treasured diver's watch smashed. Only this time, it happened so slowly that he was able to see the individual cracks appear like ice crystals forming on a window. When the glass finally shattered, his reflection stared back at him from the broken shards as they fell away into the nothingness surrounding him.

His visit to the mysterious watchmaker's shop emerged from the darkness next. He watched as Alejandra handed the memory version of him the pocket watch, her voice echoing in the gloom: *"Not yet, anyway..."*

The image floated away, instantly replaced by another and another.

His awkward meeting with Delyth joined the churning mass of fragmented memories but lasted only a second or so, before it, too, vanished. His conversation with his father appeared next – the moment he had been grounded. Chase caught a glimpse of the pain in his father's eyes – it was as if the memories had all been slowed down and zoomed in on the parts that really mattered. Each of the fragments played over and over as they surrounded him, the voices overlapping, the images blurring in and out of focus until one after another they shrank back into the blackness of the all-encompassing void.

Then a new memory appeared, but this time it was different – it was alone.

Chase squinted at the spectral scene as it took form. He was sure the ghostly figure within it was him, but he didn't recognise where he was or what was happening. It was as though the image was pixelated or blurred out. The basic shapes were there, but they seemed to be having trouble resolving themselves, like when the hands of his watches had pushed against time at school. They were there but *not there*.

He leaned in, trying to make sense of what he was seeing. The 'ghost' version of him was in a dark and cramped place and appeared to be lost or unsure. Then the penny dropped. *'Hey, I know that place – that's the study thingy with the owl, right before I woke up on the bench!'* A shadowy shape loomed over the image in the memory, but before he could see what happened next, the moment abruptly vanished – replaced by an image of the headmaster.

Chase took a step back, now he was seeing Mr Thorne telling him about the painting of the bearded pirate, Fernando Víbora Van-Quish. He watched as Thorne recounted the tale, but then something different happened, something that he was sure hadn't happened at the time... The memory version of Headmaster Thorne stopped abruptly mid-sentence as though something had caught his attention.

The images of Chase and the office faded away until only Thorne remained – alone in the darkness, his face cast in shadow. Chase gulped; it was almost like he was there together with Thorne, no longer a mere memory, but the real thing, right there in – wherever they were – with nowhere to hide.

The skinny wraith of a man prowled the void, turning this way and that, as though hunting for some unseen prey until his head abruptly snapped around and he fixed his stony gaze on Chase.

Thorne's face contorted with rage, his eyes turned as black as the void surrounding them and wiry strands of dark hair emerged from his skull like serpents. A bristling mass roiled from his face, burying it beneath a long black beard, shot through with pointed streaks of grey. He drew back his lips in a terrifying grimace, extended a pale, skeletal finger and hissed: "YOU! HOW ARE YOU DOING THIS?"

Chase fell backwards, tumbling into the darkness.

The watch clicked shut and Thorne and the void vanished at once.

Drawing breath in huge gasps, Chase clutched at his chest. He could feel his heart pounding like a jackhammer through his ribcage. He was safe, the visions had gone. He was alone in his room once more. The wall clock read 4.38pm.

MEANWHILE

Headmaster Thorne sprang to his feet so fast that his chair flew across his office and crashed to the floor. He had felt something... *something* *what*? Something... "...unexpected".

A dazzling beam of light shone out from beneath the wall of clocks, engulfing the room in a golden glow. Thorne's eyes rolled into the back of his head and his shoulders fell limp. His head lolled backwards, and he crashed to his knees. For a few moments, he stayed there, perfectly still, and silent, bathed in light, sightless and mute. He raised a bony finger and pointed at some unseen foe. "YOU!" he hissed. "HOW ARE YOU DOING THIS?"

Then, with a low moan, he grasped his head tightly between his hands and squeezed as if trying to squash his own skull. "Too much!" he howled. "Too many days. Days? Years? Is it years? When's now? Is it now?" The crazed headmaster gazed around with his blank eyes; his face twisted into a feral grimace. "The auger!" he babbled. "He sees me! It hurts! It hurts when it pulls me here and pulls me there. He has power, this one! So much power for one so young." Still on his knees, Thorne twitched and tore at himself wildly as though he was under attack from a thousand invisible wasps. "When was I this? Is this new? WHERE'S MY CHEST?" He leapt to his feet and jabbed a finger into his temple, "Where is it, Thorne?"

The once calm and controlled headmaster had been completely transformed, replaced by a crazed wild thing. He stared into the many clock faces and twisted versions of his own face stared back at him. "I won't stay in here for ever, you know!" sneered the reflections. "You're not even real, Thorne! Your time is almost over."

Like a puppet whose strings had been cut, he dropped to the floor and curled up into a ball, staring blankly into space, clutching his head. Seconds passed and his glassy eyes never blinked, his lips stayed in constant motion, chanting some silent mantra. The seconds became minutes, glistening beads of sweat broke out on his forehead and a long breath left his lips.

Then, as though some invisible switch had been flicked, Headmaster Thorne uncoiled himself, rose to his feet and smiled up at the huge painting looming over him. The bearded face of Captain Fernando Víbora Van-Quish stared down; its eyes boring into him. When he finally spoke, Thorne's voice sounded as though he had been chewing on sandpaper and broken glass: "The Connors boy is an auger! So young... I wonder..."

13

THE CHASE CHASE

"Truth – swear!" Chase placed a hand on his heart and raised three fingers. It probably wasn't the most effective way of persuading Delyth about everything that had happened with the shop and Alejandra and the pocket watch, but lunchtimes at the academy flew past so fast that every second counted – even on a Friday – so it would have to do.

"Tomorrow, old pier, midday, show me." Delyth grimaced and shovelled in a shrivelled green blob that Chase assumed was supposed to be a vegetable of some kind. He was about to protest about being grounded when she piped up: "Know grounded, *try*, I'll wait. No come, no prob. See you then, hope."

"OK, thanks, I'll try." Chase watched as she abandoned her gross so-called lunch and headed off to class. Grounded or not, he was determined to help her. After all, it was his fault she was stuck in the nightmare academy with a time-controlling maniac for a headmaster – and an appalling cook.

Three *beeps* sounded, signalling the end of lunch and, as usual, the other students all plodded off to their next lessons in silence.

"Hey, *special-case-Chase*," called a scornful voice. "I want a word with you."

Chase froze. He knew who it was straight away – Richard Pritchard, the horrendous student rep – and the unmistakeable glee in the self-important little turd's voice meant that something was up, something that would inevitably mean bad news.

"Mr Thorne wants to see you in his office, right now," he sneered. "He said it's urgent. Sounds to me like you're in for it."

The hair on the back of Chase's neck prickled and his blood ran cold. "And if I don't feel like going to see the head today, what are *you* going to do about it?"

To Chase's surprise, Pritchard didn't seem at all fazed. If anything, a faint smile had appeared in the corners of his mouth. "He said you might resist and that we were to do whatever it takes."

Pritchard's use of the word *"we"* caused Chase to look around in alarm. Sure enough, the dinner hall had emptied out completely; even the midday supervisors had vanished. The only people left were the student reps, who had tactically positioned themselves in front of all the exits and – Chase was alarmed to note – were all clutching lacrosse sticks. "You've got to be kidding me! What's the plan, hit me over the head until I agree to c... *Ouch!*"

A sharp pain sliced through Chase's head and blood sprayed from his lip as a sudden blow knocked him off his feet.

"Got it in one," laughed a girl's voice. "Get up, '*special-case*' or – even better – *don't*, so I can hit you again!"

Chase looked up to find Abigail Pansy standing over him clutching a bloodied lacrosse stick with a crazed expression on her face. He clambered to his feet, dusted himself down and rounded on her. "I'm going to the police. This is nuts! Thorne's insane, *you're* insane! This is assault."

"No, silly," Pansy cooed, smiling sweetly. "This is just a PE lesson and you're just clumsy." She rammed the end of her lacrosse stick into Chase's stomach, knocking the wind of out him. "Now *move*, or the headmaster says he'll permanently exclude that Maddocks girlfriend of yours, and make *you* spend the rest of term in detention – when *we've* finished with you that is. And that'll be detention. *Every. Single. Night.*" She leant down to Chase, who was still struggling to catch his breath. "And he promises to make them extra, *extra*-long detentions!"

Chase considered this for a moment, before doing the only thing that made sense. He held his hands up and hung his head. "OK, I'll come."

Pansy and Pritchard gave each other a smug, self-satisfied grin, which was precisely what Chase had been counting on. In one swift movement, he snatched Prichard's lacrosse stick out of his hands, spun it around like a TV Ninja and slammed the handle end straight into the fire alarm by the hall door, before plopping the netted end neatly over Pritchard's stunned face and making a dash for the kitchens.

Or at least, he tried to.

Chase watched in horror as the tiny shards of glass from the fire alarm fell to the floor in slow motion, *"What?"* He dug his feet into the hall floor and pushed as hard as his legs would allow, but it was like trying to run through syrup. Behind him, Pansy's lacrosse stick was slowly arcing through the air towards him inch by inch, her face behind it bunched up into an angry snarl.

Each step took an age.

Each second felt like an hour.

Time was slowing all around him – Thorne was at it again.

He desperately looked around for a way to escape, the only possible route would be through the kitchen, which would involve jumping over several tables and then sliding under the serving counter – all in slowed-down time while avoiding Thorne's lunatic reps – no easy task. He knew from his previous school escapes (of which there had been more than a few and that was not something he was proud of!) that school kitchens got hot from all the ovens, which meant that the doors and windows were almost always wide open, making for handy emergency exits. Part of him longed to go and try to warn Delyth, but he knew she'd be safer in a classroom surrounded by witnesses than doing a runner with him, so he abandoned the idea and charged, as quickly as one can charge in slow-motion, towards the kitchen.

The first table jump came up after what seemed like minutes – but was only three steps from where he had begun. Slimy grey jelly coated the tabletop making it easier for him to slide across its grimy surface and giving him a good momentum boost towards table number two, where a particularly large rep had got a good head start on him and was preparing to cut him off. Seeing this, Chase made a last-minute feint and, as the muscly meathead tried to intercept his leap over the table, he turned the leap into a dive and rolled underneath instead. Disgusting chewed-up peas and brussels sprouts squashed all over his blazer as he thundered along the floor like a human cannonball, taking the rep's feet out from under him.

Fighting down the urge to stop and celebrate, Chase leapt to his feet – which was an odd thing to experience in slow motion. His stomach churned and the bitter taste of vomit filled his mouth. The effects of the super-slowed-down time coupled with the disgusting food debris had started him retching and heaving, which gave him an extremely unpleasant idea as he slowly ran towards the last rep between him and the serving counter and the promise of escape beyond. If Thorne could make time into a weapon. Then he could do the same with what was about to happen...

The last rep was a tall and obscenely handsome chap with a glowing tan, who looked like he had walked off the set of an American high-school movie. Clearly enjoying the effects of the slowed time, he heroically flicked his floppy blonde hair out of his face and flashed a confident grin filled with perfect teeth. A grin that quickly faded when, instead trying to dodge him, his quarry simply launched himself straight into him and latched on like a baby monkey. Chase smiled down at the confused jock, heaved a few times, gave him a cheeky wink, and then violently threw up straight into the great lunk's face.

Glistening chunks of slimy, second-hand carrots splattered down the rep's tanned cheeks, while the remnants of at least one bilious sprout found its way into his gaping mouth. The disgusting sight was made even worse by the fact that the entire revolting scene was played out in slow motion, meaning that the overconfident rep had plenty of time to savour the texture of someone else's semi-digested lunch slipping down his throat. Satisfied that the rep was suitably distracted, Chase let go of his retching victim, wiped his chin, and slid under the serving counter to freedom.

Time returned to its normal flow as he entered the kitchen and made for a wide-open window that was just the perfect size for a teenage boy to jump through. He didn't waste time on caution, and simply dived through headfirst and was grateful to land in a stinky, but well-placed recycling bin. Some 20 normal-length seconds later, he was out of the school gates and heading as far from the "Academy for Raising Standards in Exceptionalism" as fast as his legs could carry him, all the while praying that Delyth would be OK.

14

I KNEW IT!

S afely tucked away in his favourite clifftop hiding place, at least a dozen plans ran through Chase's mind as he glowered forlornly down at the waves far below. Most of them involved running away and starting a new life somewhere else. He spent a good 10 minutes convinced that going to the police was his best option, until he realised that he didn't exactly have the best reputation with the local constabulary, even at the best of times. If he went to the police station claiming that his headmaster could control time and had had him beaten up because he'd trespassed in his memory-vision thing, he would probably be arrested for wasting police time. That or seem like an absolute maniac and end up being banged up for life in some sort of institution. Not that it mattered... *When Dad and Max find out, I'm probably going to end up locked in my room until I'm 30 anyway.*

"First things first," he announced to no one in particular, but saying it out loud and standing up and placing his hands on his hips made him feel more in control. "Go home, get that pocket watch, take it back to the shop and ask that Alejandra lady what the heck is going on!" He stomped off home trying to convince himself that he was brimming with resolve.

It didn't take too long to get the pocket watch. Thankfully Dad was in his studio playing guitar with his headphones on, as always, making it easy to sneak in and out unseen. Grateful for at least one small victory, Chase made his way back to where the owl had led him to the fantastical shop, Meridian...

Only it wasn't there.

He stared at the empty spot trying and failing to feel surprised instead of irritated. "Obviously it's gone," he vented. "I knew it! I mean, it was blatantly going to be gone!"

There was nothing but barren, innocuous scrubland where the clockmaker's shop had stood only a few days earlier. "Mysterious disappearing shop – it's literally the oldest cliché in the book!" He threw his hands up in despair. "Now what am I supposed to do?"

With the metaphorical wind utterly removed from his metaphorical sails, and feeling very literally useless, Chase spun on the spot like a dog making its bed, *harrumphed* a few times to get his frustration out, and then sat down right there in the street to think. He took out the mysterious pocket watch and peered at its decorated case for a moment, pondering the likelihood of being drawn into another weird memory-vision thing again if he opened it. "Stuff it," he glanced around, took a deep breath, and opened the watch again...

Nothing happened.

He breathed out. "Anti-climax much." This time there was no swirling mass of memories, no haunting choir – just the inside of a watch with some strange writing in it... and a dark shadow that had fallen over him. He looked up, half expecting to see Thorne looming over him, but the shadow wasn't people-shaped, it was shop-shaped.

It was back!

Right where it had been before, on the exact same spot that had been empty seconds earlier, stood the odd little shop. It was exactly as he had left it, right down to the sign on the door declaring it closed for lunch. Chase rubbed his eyes and blinked several times. The shop stayed put. "Hey!" He snapped the watch shut and leapt to his feet, ready to bang on the little wooden door for all he was worth.

The shop disappeared.

"What the..?"

He waved a hand through the space where the shop had been. It passed through the air, but not smoothly. It was strange, nothing appeared amiss, but something felt weird, for sure. He took a few steps on to the scrubland. It looked normal enough, just like every other disused little spot in every other little town – a few weeds, some cracked old paving slabs, a lolly stick, some gravel, maybe a bit of broken glass, a whole lot of nothing. But the longer he stood there, the more the air grew colder than it had been on the pavement just inches away, and the more his tummy felt a little bit – iffy.

"Wait a minute," he stepped back on to the pavement, looked around and pulled out the watch once more. Once again, he drew a deep breath, and this time gritted his teeth for good measure. Slowly, he flipped back the latch holding the pocket watch closed.

Nothing happened.

Then, as gingerly as he could, he slipped a fingernail into the crack in the casing and carefully eased it open.

The shop came back.

"NO WAY!" he closed the watch and, before he could blink, the shop was gone.

He opened the watch, and the shop returned.

He closed the watch, and the shop vanished.

He opened the watch, mouth agape, and the shop returned once more.

He closed the watch with a *snap*, and the shop stopped being there again.

"OK, last time!" He opened the watch again, and once more, the odd little shop popped into existence. This time, he decided to try the door. It was firmly locked, so he tried peering through the tiny lead windows, but they were too dusty and warped to see anything. He tried banging on the door for several minutes, but no one answered, so he *harrumphed* again and took a moment to think. It occurred to him to try standing where he thought would be an empty spot inside the shop while it was scrubland, and *then* opening the watch, to see if he materialised inside. But it also occurred to him that, if he was wrong, or the floor level was different, he could end up stuck inside a wall, or the floor or the counter, or mushed to pieces in the cogs of the giant clock that lay beneath the transparent floor. The thought gave him the shivers, so he decided to study the watch's innards for clues, which was exactly what Alejandra had told him to do all along – and there was no doubting now that she was somehow involved in the whole messed-up-time debacle in some way.

The inside of the pocket watch was in much worse condition than the outside. The face itself was relatively unremarkable, being of age-yellowed white with roman numerals around its edge. The centre bore no maker's name, which was unusual, but there was certainly nothing to suggest the watch was in any way capable of the bizarre feat of making a shop appear and disappear. Simple gold hands matched the numerals and a thick coating of dust had collected inside the cover, obscuring some of the inscription that had been engraved there. He scratched away at the grime with his fingernail, but it quickly became apparent that even if he could clean it up, whatever the words said, it wasn't in any language he recognised.

"Ti...po esp...da kaq...nqa kay esc...oyki k.. hun"

15

THE LIBRARY

For someone who had grown accustomed to having the entirety of human knowledge available in his back pocket, Chase found not having a phone truly frustrating. Especially when trying to decode half a sentence of some unknown language that was buried under grime inside an old pocket watch that acted as an on/off switch for a mysterious disappearing shop. He racked his teenage brain for several minutes trying to work out how on earth he could find out what the inscription said, and then it occurred to him...

A brilliant idea!

An idea so ingenious that he imagined no other teenager in the history of teenagers had ever come up with such a ground-breaking concept! He would do what those ancient forefathers who had come before had done, long ago in the mists of almost-forgotten history...

He would go... to a library! Like an old person!

Feeling super-pleased with his radical plan, he set off to the library with a spring in his step – until he realised, he had no idea if Bisby even *had* a library, much less where to find it... He wasn't really a library sort of guy.

Ten minutes later, after asking 10 different people, eight of whom turned out to be bewildered tourists, he set off again in a somewhat slightly less springy fashion and following some vague directions that a kindly old lady thought *might* get him to a library... or possibly a boy's school. Some 20 minutes and a few of Bisby's steep hills later, he was pleasantly surprised to discover that Bisby *did* have a library, and that the old lady had been right... on both counts.

At the end of a particularly steep and narrow hill, he finally came across a curious old building which, like most buildings in Bisby, was made from the local stone. The entrance was a large wooden door flanked by two mean-looking lion statues, each clutching a thick book in its giant paws and peering down on those who dared to enter. There was something about their stony eyes that made Chase feel uneasy, but he knew they wouldn't eat him, because they were statues and statues don't tend to eat people, or at least not in other towns – in Bisby, however, death by statue consumption was starting to seem not that unlikely! A rusty plaque above the door announced that the library had been built in 1842 as the "Bisby School for Errant Boys". The entire building exuded a distinctly unwelcoming air – as either a school *or* a library. Even in the brilliant summer sunshine, its crumbling façade remained stubbornly hidden in shade. With an involuntary shiver, Chase stepped between the lions and into the gloomy interior.

The old wooden floor creaked beneath his feet like in a cheesy old horror movie, and dusty old chandeliers tinkled above his head. Blood-red wallpaper with fuzzy patterns in dark maroon covered the walls. Each side of the corridor was lined with mould-green lampshades finished off with little golden tassels that dangled and spiralled around hypnotically.

Music was playing from somewhere – it sounded as if it was coming from the floor above and trickling down through the knotholes in the wooden ceiling. It wasn't like any music he had heard before. For a start, there weren't any words, it was just a strange, tinny, swirly sound that crackled and jumped and sounded more as if it was emanating from a long tube than being played through a speaker. It made him feel drowsy and reminded him of the old Ferris wheel on the seafront, not the unfinished new reproduction, but its antique predecessor that had decided to malfunction one night and wreck half the town.

"Do you need something, dear?" A thin, elderly lady appeared from nowhere, making Chase leap back in alarm. She had a pile of white hair stacked on top of her head in a tight bun, weird, triangular glasses perched on her inhumanly pointed nose and a mouth not entirely unlike a dog's bottom. "You must be young Chase Connors, then. I was wondering when you'd show up." She eyed him up and down suspiciously for a moment. "You've grown." The hairs on the back of Chase's neck stood up – he had no idea who this woman was, let alone how she knew him or his name, and it made him nervous. "I'm Mrs Crisp, the librarian," she smiled, revealing a handful of yellowed teeth. "Follow me, follow me, no time for dawdling, Master Connors, summer won't last for ever, the leaves will turn before you can blink." The strange old lady turned on her heels and marched off at a surprisingly sprightly pace, leaving Chase trotting along behind her, wondering what on earth was going on.

"Mrs Crisp," he called after her, starting to feel distinctly impatient and somewhat worn out from his already very long day. "Do you have a computer I can use?" He yawned and rubbed his eyes, that damn music was so annoying. *Why was he there again? Oh right, the computer.* "I just need to find out what something means, and I don't have my phone with me."

"Tell me, have you ever seen one of these before?" Chase blinked, trying to fight away the sudden drowsiness that was threatening to overwhelm him. Mrs Crisp was holding a bizarre contraption in front of his face that she had apparently produced from out of nowhere. It looked like an old-fashioned table lamp poking out of a cake tin full of tiny mirrors and faded old picture cards. "This is called a 'praxinoscope', Master Connors, and it's a storyteller like no other – look, watch closely!"

"I'm not here for stories Mrs Crisp, I only need to translate something... please." A lightness had taken over Chase's head. It reminded him of when he had boasted that he could hold his breath for over two minutes and had been called out on it. He'd been far too belligerent to quit and had subsequently ended up winning five pounds and then fainting underwater and having to be rescued – but on a positive note, that was the five pounds that had finally won him the Robowatch.

"The praxinoscope is perfect for translations, too." Mrs Crisp smiled her disturbing smile again, and it looked as though her lips were moving in slow motion, her voice sounded all slow and deep. "Watch it spin. Watch it spin."

"Not here, too," thought Chase. *"Is time broken everywhere in Bisby now?"*

Unable to resist her command, he peered intently at the praxinoscope as it started to spin. "Lose yourself in its tales of wonder and mystery!" cackled Mrs Crisp. "Lose yourself!"

He stares back at himself, an image reflected in a mirror with an onyx frame. But the glass is not still, it eddies and churns around him like the bubbles underwater when he held his breath for too long. An owl appears on his reflection's shoulder, its yellow eyes burning like the sun...

...A vicious sun casts its light down on the raised faces of a thousand men and women as they reach to the heavens. A stepped pyramid looms over the massed throng. It is of gargantuan proportions and draped in brightly coloured fabrics and gleaming golden artifacts of all shapes and sizes. Hundreds of people swarm eagerly up the monolith like ants, each clutching something close to their chest. At the pyramid's peak, high among the clouds, a tall man in gaudy robes and wearing a heavy and intricately decorated headdress holds his hands above his head. He wields a glowing crystal, somehow hewn into the shape of an hourglass, housed in a solid gold frame. A serene golden light erupts from within the gemstone as he leads the vast assembly in chants of: "Inti, Inti!"

The light fades, the pyramid still stands, but now it is damaged and worn. The golden artifacts are gone, replaced by bodies lying still. Now it is blood that drapes the steps and greasy black smoke that shrouds its summit. Armoured men wave swords aloft and the sky darkens with arrows. Voices scream and a man with a feather in his cap raises the hourglass crystal in triumph...

...A lifeless hand still clutches the golden frame, but the hourglass-shaped crystal imprisoned within is stained with red now. A grand palace is swarmed by angry men. They emerge carrying a body with a feathered cap. A wiry man with a long black beard prises the crystal from the dead man's grasp.

...In the darkness, time passes. Hundreds of years fly past in an instant. There is joy and rage and love and loss in such measure as to overwhelm the capacity of any single lifetime. Hope rises – it is beautiful, with skin as pale as snowfall and lips as red as blood. But greed takes the form of a hooded serpent and turns on hope and all is lost. As hope retreats, the snake coils around the red-stained crystal, its eyes narrow and accusing...

...Darkness engulfs everything. There are days and nights and the world changes. But hope stays hidden. A blade pierces the dark, sharp enough to cut through emptiness itself. A scream rings out and a flash of golden light shatters the blackness for an instant as two shards of crystal fall, glittering like rain in the night sky.

Hope retreats again and the snake coils even tighter...

...A figure works in silence, nimble fingers placing cog into gear into pinion. Piece by piece, a familiar object takes form – a pocket watch, finely decorated and smooth like a worn pebble. At its heart, a tiny shard of blood-red crystal. A face is placed, a casing is sealed around it, and the crystal is hidden away.

Words appear, burning with golden light and written in a language spoken by the dead...

. . .

...Words burned into Chase's retina, a ghostly echo of what was. Words that fade away as his heart pounds in his chest and sweat drenches his forehead.

"Sorry I couldn't be more use, dear, I never did understand computers, curious objects if you ask me. And I'm quite sure that this one must be an antique by now!"

"What?" Chase blinked, his head was fuzzy and discombobulated, it felt as though he was waking from a dream.

"Don't say *what*, dear, say *pardon*."

The world took form and shape around Chase; Mrs Crisp was staring at him blankly. The room was different, too, the corridor with its creaky floor and tasselled wall lights had gone and there was no sign of the praxinoscope. He was standing in the middle of a large room filled with shelves of musty-smelling books, each wrapped in a wrinkled plastic dust cover and tagged with a number. An ancient computer sat on a beige steel trolley in one corner, a single red light blinking away on its equally beige casing. Next to it lay a pile of dusty old floppy discs and an antiquated printer.

Chase became dimly aware that he was holding something and opened his hand to find he was clutching a strip of old-fashioned printer paper with a single sentence etched on its faint green lines...

"When time is a sword, let this be your shield."

16

PAGE INTENTIONALLY LEFT BLANK

"I'm so glad you came to see me, Mr Connors, I'm certain that we can have this whole misunderstanding cleared up in no time at all. Please, take a seat." Headmaster Thorne slid a chair towards Chase's father.

Jon Connors looked around the office, noting that a pale girl was sitting at a table with a stricken expression on her face. She was wearing a uniform, so had to be a pupil, and was surrounded by blank sheets of lined paper. She had paid him no attention at all and appeared to be deep in thought, to the point where the pen she clutched in her hand hadn't moved since he had walked in. In fact, he wasn't sure if she had even blinked yet. Unsure what to make of her, he decided she might be in trouble of some type, so gave her an awkward attempt at a sympathetic smile that went unacknowledged.

"I'm afraid that there was an unfortunate incident in school today involving Chase," intoned the headmaster, taking a seat and pouring himself a glass of water.

Jon sighed, his breath frosting in the cold air of Thorne's

office. He glanced at the curiously still young woman, thinking it extremely unprofessional of the head to have her around while discussing matters to do with another pupil – he was sure it was against the rules. The girl still hadn't moved; her face was fixed in place staring into the middle distance. "Well, whatever he's done, maybe we could discuss it in private? I'm sure it..."

"I think you misunderstand," smiled Thorne. "Chase was the victim here. I'm sorry to say that a deeply... *damaged* pupil of ours attacked your son and then upset him further by misinforming him that he was in serious trouble with me. To make matters worse, they compounded the situation by setting off the fire alarm and claiming that Chase was responsible. I would like to assure you that the pupil in question has been severely reprimanded."

The head's words jumbled together in Jon's head. He found it impossible not to be distracted by the presence of the odd girl. Was it her? Had she attacked Chase? Was that why she was here – some sort of restorative justice situation? Surely it was wildly inappropriate to have her in the room.

In his peripheral vision he could see that she was still utterly stationary, the only way he could tell she was even breathing was the faint hint of fog at her lips. It was plain weird, as if someone had pressed a "pause" button on her. "Where is Chase now?" he demanded. "Is he alright? I want to see him."

The head sipped at his water, in no apparent rush. "He is fine, the injuries he received were slight at best. But I'm afraid that in his panic, Chase left the premises without permission, and I am deeply concerned for his welfare. We have called the phone number on file for him, but there is no answer, I wonder... have you heard from him at all?"

Jon leapt to his feet, aghast that the head was being so calm under the circumstances. "You could have said that first! He doesn't have his phone, I confiscated it after *you* gave him detention on his first day! And now he's been attacked and you're not out looking for him?" He looked over at the girl, who even now remained as immobile and impassive as ever. "What kind of weird school are you running here, Thorne? Have you even called the police?"

Thorne rose to his feet and slapped an official-looking document on the desk. "I assure you that the relevant authorities *have* been contacted, and I have lots of people out looking for Chase right now. Please, why don't you complete this form for me while we wait for news. It grants us permission to bring him back in a school vehicle if we find him."

Jon was raging, the last thing he wanted to do was fill in a form. He needed to call Max and get out looking for his son, but his stomach was beginning to churn and the cold in the office was so intense it was starting to hurt his head – it felt like a bout of intense pins and needles, but inside his brain.

"Please," Thorne clicked a pen and slid the document across his desk as Chase's father slumped back into his chair clutching at his stomach. "It will help us all and will only take a moment – you have my word!"

His head swimming, a strange compulsion to comply overcame him and Jon snatched the pen and looked at the first page, it read: 'This page intentionally left blank.'

Time ground to a halt as he searched for the meaning there.

Thorne admired his prizes, Delyth Maddocks and the boy's father, both trapped in the same never-ending instant. An email to the girl's parents about an after-school study club would buy him a few hours to find the boy without arousing suspicion, but the father was an unknown quantity. It might be that a *tragic accident* would befall them both before the day was out. "Now then, Chase Connors," he hissed. "Time to find out what's really going on here."

17

A LONG TIME AGO

Chase flicked the latch, and the pocket watch sprang open. As before, the patch of scrubland vanished, replaced by the fantastical shop, Meridian. Only this time, the sign on the door was gone, although the door itself remained firmly shut. "Hey!" He pounded his fists against the door and rattled the knob. "I know you're in there!" He took two steps back and ran at the heavy wooden door, landing as hard a kick as he could manage, but it didn't budge. Next, he looked around for something to throw and settled on the only available object, a rock the size of his fist. "Last chance!" he banged on the door again. "Open the damn door or this comes through the window." No answer was forthcoming, so he pulled back his arm, waited a moment and then hurled the small rock straight at one of the tiny square windowpanes.

The glass shimmered for a moment, and the rock passed straight through, vanishing without so much as a sound. "What the?" He poked the window, it was still there, fully intact, and definitely "there" – he could feel the cool glass beneath his fingertips. "Right, that's it!" He placed the pocket watch on the floor and raised a foot above it. "Open the damn door and tell me what the hell is going on or I grind this stupid watch into dust right now. Then I'll chuck whatever's left into the harbour, I swear I will!"

Nothing happened.

"Three!"

He gritted his teeth.

"Two!"

He glared at the door; his jaw tightened.

"One!"

The door opened and a stunning young woman appeared. She was easily the most beautiful human being Chase had ever seen. She was also extremely familiar, and it stopped him dead in his tracks. "Alejandra? Is that you? How are you... you... you're... young?"

"Not as young as you!" she snapped, beckoning to him. "Now you'd better come inside and stop making a scene before the whole world notices us!"

Chase picked up the watch and followed her into the shop, which faded from view, leaving only the empty scrubland behind.

"I suppose I should tell you the truth – please sit down." Alejandra took a seat behind the counter and poured herself a glass of velvety red drink from an unusually tall bottle. Her shoulders slumped and she sighed deeply.

Chase crossed his arms and tried not to think about the long drop underneath his feet into the depths of the underfloor clock. "What's going on here? How are you young now? And what do you know about my headmaster messing with time?"

"Tea?" She reached beneath the counter and produced a silver tray bearing a steaming pot of tea and two fine china cups and saucers.

"No."

"Oh, coffee then?" She replaced the tray and at once pulled out another. This time, the tray bore a full cafetière, two homely-looking mugs and a bowl of sugar lumps.

"NO!"

Looking disappointed, Alejandra once again reached under the counter. "Sangría, then – no, too young." Seeming perplexed, she reached under once more and produced a tartan flask with a yellowed plastic cup for a lid. "How about a nice cup of..." She studied the flask for a moment. "Actually, I have no idea what's in there, or how long it's been in there for. Shall we find out together? It'll be fun!" She unscrewed the lid and peered into the flask before retching and shoving it back under the counter. "Perhaps not today. Let's look at the cakes, shall we?"

"Answer my questions or the watch gets it," Chase said simply.

This took the wind out of Alejandra's sails. She shrugged, downed some more of the red drink, and silently studied him for an awkwardly long time. "Fine," she announced eventually. "Sit."

Chase plonked himself down on a rickety-looking old three-legged stool as she took another long swig of the drink.

"My name is Alejandra Rosamunda Vela, and this is my shop. I'm young today but sometimes I'm old and sometimes I'm in the middle – age has a middle, you know. That's how time is around here. Meridian isn't merely a shop, you see. I suppose it's more of a... hiding place," she declared, as though that explained everything. "The watch I gave you shares its... *heart* with that one, down there." She indicated towards the huge clock that lay beneath them.

Chase looked down and a wave of vertigo ran up his body making him shiver. "You get used to it," she said with a smile, seeing his reaction. "They aren't actual hearts, obviously, rather they're both fragments, parts of a larger..."

"Let me guess – crystal." Chase interrupted. "A blood-red crystal shaped like an hourglass, kept inside a golden frame that was stolen from the Incas by the Spanish and then stolen from them by some other dude with a big beard, probably called 'something Van-Quish' – cool name by the way. The crystal, I'm guessing, can control time somehow and the big part of it is being kept in the headmaster's office in my school because... well, actually I don't know why. But how am I doing so far?"

Alejandra's jaw dropped open; her dark eyes were wide and glittering with emotion. "What a wonderful feeling!" she sniffled. "I've not felt surprised in decades at least, maybe longer. Thank you, Chase. How on earth have you come to be so well informed already?"

He pondered how to explain the bizarre visions he had experienced in the library, before deciding to keep things simple. "Library... vision... spinny thing... probably magic, I'm assuming at this point."

Alejandra appeared unfazed by this revelation. "Hmm, *more* magic? You're probably right. How curious this town is. I'm sure you've noticed by now that Bisby by the Sea is prone to that sort of thing?"

"I had spotted it, yes."

"It isn't a coincidence, Chase, just like you finding Meridian was no coincidence, either."

"Go on." Chase leaned in towards her. "Because I've landed myself in a whole heap of trouble escaping from a lynching at school and now I'm hiding out in a vanishing shop with a lady who can change her age, so, believe me, I'm listening."

Alejandra's face sagged; her eyes sank into their sockets,

deep lines encircled them, and her jaw lost its sharpness. Age crept over her, and she winced as though in pain.

Chase realised that his face must have betrayed his shock, as she clasped his hand in hers and smiled. "Don't be alarmed. As I said, sudden aging is just something that happens in here. Time comes and goes in strange ways in Meridian, but don't worry, you haven't been in here nearly long enough for it to happen to you. It takes a long time, a really long time. You might feel a little dizzy and sick for a bit is all."

"Yeah, the same as at the school." Chase nodded. "How long *have* you been in here, Alejandra?"

Her eyes clouded over, a grey pall washing away the intense darkness that had burned there only moments before. "I don't even know any more, Chase. I can leave if I need to, now and then, when my body is young. But if I'm away too long, then time starts to catch up with me faster than I can outrun it. If I were to be away from Meridian for too long, I'd be dust in the wind before the day was out."

"What are you? An alien? A time traveller? Incan? Time-travelling alien-Inca?"

Age relaxed its grip on the woman and years fell away, her face softened and the lines around her eyes retreated. "Alien – no. Time-traveller – no, well, a *bit* perhaps, but not in the sense you mean, anyway. But your 'spinny-thing library magic' was correct in what it showed you. I *am* what you'd call Incan. Or at least, I was once."

A haunted expression overtook the woman, aging her almost as much as Meridian's unpredictable passage of time had done. "A very long time ago I lived far from here," she said sadly. "Deep in a jungle on the slopes of a beautiful mountain, under the gaze of our benevolent gods. I had such a happy life there with my tribe and my family. We had all that we needed.

That and treasures and magics long lost to the world you know."

"The crystal is magic?" asked Chase.

"Yes," she replied, with pain in her eyes. "The crystal's magic is as old as the universe itself. It was a gift from our gods, born in the heart of the first star, back before time even existed. Its power meant we had all the time we needed to worship, and even more besides."

She took a long swig from the tall bottle, paused, and then took another, clearly readying herself for recounting a difficult memory. "Life changed the day I met a man wandering in the jungles at the foot of our mountain. He was like no other man I had ever seen. His skin was worn and tough like leather, but his eyes were so kind that I trusted him at once. He was alone and injured, claiming to be an explorer seeking the edge of the known world."

A darkness descended over Alejandra; it was so intense that Chase felt the hairs on his arms stand up. "The pirate, Fernando Van-Quish?" he asked. "His painting is in my head-master's office. He said he had gifts from the gods, long life, and the power of persuasion – he's kinda scary looking?"

"Yes." A tear rolled down her cheek and she dabbed it away with her sleeve. "Forgive me, it's one thing to hold a memory to yourself, but another to share it out loud. Anyway, as I was saying, I trusted him straight away – like a fool – so I took him back to my people and nursed him back to health. My family and the village leaders were angry at first and tried to send him away, but soon they grew to trust him also." She shook her head sadly. "If only I had listened to them."

"I'm sorry this is upsetting you," said Chase. "We can stop if you like."

Alejandra pressed her hands together and smiled wistfully at him. "You are a kind boy, Chase, but it's best you understand. You see, as I nursed him back to health, Fernando and I fell deeply in love and the years slipped past us. Thanks to our wonderful crystal, time in our village ran differently from in the outside world. Fernando and I spent decades together, just he and I and our love for each other." She hesitated and took a long swig from the tall bottle. "The only thing I loved more than that man was Inti himself."

"Inti?"

"The most important of our gods. My people believed it was he who created the crystal and gifted it to our forefathers, who then contained it within a frame made of precious metals. The crystal was our most valued treasure."

"Why, what was it for?" Chase asked.

"Inti understood that the love our people held for him was greater than the number of hours in a day or the days in a year. The crystal – in your language it would be called the *'Time Driver'* – could alter time, allowing us to worship him for longer each day. It was a true blessing, until it became a curse. You see, I never paid attention to how obsessed my Fernando had become with our Time Driver. I was blinded by my love for him and having more time with him every day felt like heaven."

Chase smiled at her. "Yeah, like my dad somehow never sees the mess Max leaves in the kitchen when he's been fixing old car parts in there."

She raised a single eyebrow. "Erm, yes, a bit like that... perhaps. Anyway, in time, Fernando persuaded me that he had to leave our village and return to his own world. For years he begged and pleaded with me to come. The way he described it made it sound like such a wonderful place, full of sights beyond anything I had seen on my mountain. I suppose in some ways he was right. Anyway, like the fool I was, I packed my sword and went with him. It left my family heartbroken, and I never forgave myself for that. It wasn't until much later that I discovered Van-Quish had betrayed my people. He'd revealed the location of our home to an army desperate to take our gold and our magics for themselves. He hadn't been looking for the edge of the world at all when I met him. He was looking for us the whole time."

"Then why did he stay with you for such a long time?" asked Chase.

She stared off into space for a moment, before giving a long sigh. "Our love was real, Chase; I believe that much. But as for why he did what he did, the truth is I don't really know. He's a unique magical being all of his own, thanks to his gifts from the gods. Time moves differently for him. I imagine his perception of time is so different to our own that we can't hope to understand how he thinks."

Chase rubbed his stomach, the constant nausea from being around time changes was starting to become extremely unpleasant and talking about love made him uncomfortable at the best of times. "Amazing story," he said. "Really amazing, but what's it got to do with a disappearing shop and my school headmaster controlling time hundreds of years later?"

Alejandra went for another swig before realising that the bottle was empty. With a shrug, she reached under the counter and pulled out the tray with the teapot, which was somehow still piping hot, and went about pouring herself a cup. "Well, that's where things get a bit... vague. Tea?"

Chase shook his head and pointed at his stomach. "No thanks, I'm a bit *off*."

"Ah yes," she grimaced. "Time-shifting will do that to you. Anyway, Fernando and I came to his new world and lived together for many happy years before I learned of his betrayal. We travelled the globe and had more adventures than most people could dream of experiencing in a dozen lifetimes. But unbeknownst to me, it was all funded by his payment for leading the Spanish army to my family home. I suppose our life of adventure was why it took me longer to realise than I should that, away from the effects of the Time Driver, age was catching up with me – but it never touched my Fernando. He barely aged a day in all our years together. His beautiful beard hid it for a while. He called it an unexplained miracle how time seemed to have such little effect on him, but he had noticed the ageing in me, of course, both in my health and in my looks. It was this that drove him to reclaim the Time Driver from its hiding place in the palace of the man who had slain my people. Fernando had him murdered and brought me the Time Driver as a prize, claiming its powers would allow us to be together for all time. I'm sorry to say that only *then* did I realise, Chase, that he was not the man I had thought him to be. One by one, the pieces of the puzzle fell into place and the full extent of his betrayal was revealed to me. The man I knew as Fernando Van-Quish – the same man you now know as Headmaster Thorne – was a traitorous, murdering pirate. Nothing more than a mercenary with a bizarre gift of long life and the power to bend the will of others."

Chase's head felt like it would pop as he tried to process what she had said. "Wait... what? Hang on... so you're telling me that my headmaster, here in Bisby, *today* – Mr Thorne – *is* Van-Quish? Actual hundreds-of-years-old pirate dude Fernando Van-Quish? Not his great-grandson or something? But the *actual* guy? And you're his long-lost Incan love. That's impossible!"

He put his head in his hands and spoke through his fingers in a muffled voice: "But seeing as I'm literally sitting here in a shop that comes and goes, and this is Bisby and crazy stuff happens here pretty much every single day, I'm going to go along with it for now! Go on, what did you do when you found out what he'd done?"

Alejandra laughed. "I knew there was something special about you. Chase. Well, what I did was run. I took my sword, and I used all the skills I had learnt from our adventures together, and I ran. It drove him mad, and it broke both our hearts. Even after I found out what he'd done and who he really was, I still loved him. I suppose that's why when, after years of planning and watching from afar, I finally caught him unawares, I still couldn't use this."

She reached under the counter once more and produced a gleaming golden sword, which she promptly dropped to the countertop with a *clang*, sending sugar cubes flying in all directions. The weapon hummed and vibrated from the impact, Chase leapt out his stool and eyed it with suspicion. "Is that thing real? It sounds like it's whispering, or singing... or both, I can't tell!"

"Probably both," Alejandra was quite unperturbed by the presence of a singing sword. "It was forged from the same metal as the frame that contains the Time Driver. There's old magic in that sword, the purest kind, this is what I used to slice apart the crystal at the heart of the Time Driver – instead of slicing apart Fernando, I might add."

"You did *what* with it?" Chase slid back on to his stool, keeping his eyes firmly fixed on the blade that he was quite sure could slice him in two.

"After I finished being afraid of who Fernando really was, I got sad, and then eventually, I got tired of being sad and became angry instead. I changed my appearance and name and tracked Van-Quish, or *Thorne* as he calls himself now, around the globe for years. I kidded myself that I would kill him for what he'd done to my people. The invaders that he sent wiped them all out, you know, Chase. They murdered everyone I knew and destroyed our entire civilisation, all thanks to Fernando and his greed. But when I finally had my chance to kill him and take my revenge, I couldn't do it, so I lunged for the crystal instead, hoping that damaging it would stop him. It split apart and I managed to escape with my life and two crystal shards. It was something at least, and the damage left the Time Driver less powerful."

"I hate to be the bearer of bad news," said Chase. "But I've been on the wrong end of it and it still feels pretty powerful to me."

"It is," she agreed, nodding gravely. "Far too powerful for one man. The Time Driver's power was meant to be used by hundreds of people – sparingly. Even damaged, it's too much to be wielded by a single person and my Fernando was a fool, a greedy fool who had spent decades alone with it with no real understanding of its purpose. The sands of time endlessly shifting around him, along with his gift of long life, meant that his brain got more and more muddled up and he slowly forgot who he was. By the time I got to him he wasn't himself anymore. It was as though *my* Fernando had been lost, buried like one of his treasure caches, concealed deep down inside himself."

"Wait," said Chase. "You're saying Thorne *doesn't know* he's Van-Quish?"

She hesitated, seeming to struggle to find a way to explain. "It's complicated," she said eventually. "As far as I can tell, he does... and he doesn't. Let me put it this way, have you ever had a little voice inside your head that makes you do something even when you know it's a terrible idea?"

Chase thought about this for a moment. He thought about his first explosion in the science lab, and his second, and third, and fourth and fifth. And then he thought about all the other times he'd followed the little voice in his head that told him to do stupid things. "Yes," he replied, deciding not to go into details. "Yes, I have."

"Well then," she smiled. "Imagine if that little voice was the *real* you, buried deep down, lost inside your own mind, but always there, whispering to you in your quietest moments. Hiding in the darkness that lives in us all."

Chase gulped and shuffled around on his stool, suddenly uncomfortable in more ways than one.

"Anyway," she continued. "After seeing what he had become, and damaging the Time Driver, I took the shards and went back to keeping my distance and watching him from afar – as I still am today. Now and then I lose track of him, and he disappears, but he's never too hard to find these days, especially since he started gravitating towards Bisby time and time again, as though something here keeps calling him back. Every few years, he starts a new life with a new name and tries to use the Time Driver to exert power or influence of some kind. And every time we find a way to stop him. Or he forgets who he is, and the cycle begins again. The irony is that people trust him – it's another part of his so-called 'gift', along with his long life. If he would only abandon the Time Driver, he might find the good in himself, but he won't. He guards it jealously and anyone who tries to interfere with it, or his plans, always ends up..." A dark cloud seemed to descend over her. "...In a bad way."

A shiver ran up Chase's spine and he considered what she had said, letting it all sink in. "OK," he said finally. "Two more questions: Firstly, you said *'we'* just then, you said: *'We* find a way to stop him.' Who's *'we'*? And secondly, why's he in a school now? What can he possibly hope to achieve by controlling time in a *school*?"

Alejandra returned the sword to its home under the shop counter and stood up. "I think it's time for the tour."

18

THE FOREVER PEOPLE

"Come with me," Alejandra sprang to her feet and showed Chase to a dusty old grandfather clock nestling in a corner. It was so unremarkable that he hadn't even noticed it before – it was more the sort of thing that would be found languishing in just about any old junk shop, rather than the fantastical wonderland that was Meridian.

The tatty old clock's true purpose became apparent, the moment that Alejandra opened its casing to reveal a hidden staircase that vanished off down into darkness. She trotted off down the narrow steps without hesitation. "Well, come on, then," she called back to him. "What are you waiting for? I thought you *liked* messing about inside clocks!"

Somewhat bemused at yet another unexpected turn of events, Chase gingerly picked his way down the creaky old steps after her. "This place gets weirder by the second," he muttered, swiping away cobwebs as the darkness consumed him.

. . .

It took several minutes to make their way down the steep staircase, and during the long descent Chase realised that the stomach pain and nausea that had plagued him ever since entering Meridian had eased. "My tummy's much better down here," he said. "I don't feel nearly as sick."

"Good," replied Alejandra, who had become younger once more. "Sickness and nausea are side-effects of the whole 'time manipulation' thing. Speaking of which, a warning before we go any further – you might find this place a bit... unsettling."

Chase immediately saw what she meant. They had emerged into a large, circular chamber that appeared to have been grown rather than built, creating the impression that they were inside a vast hollowed-out tree. He craned his neck to see how high up it went, but there was no way to see the ceiling, as the mechanisms of the giant clock at the centre of Meridian floated in the air above him. "How is that thing staying up?" he asked, gazing up at the strange sight. "It just floats there!"

"Time," replied Alejandra bluntly. "Time keeps it there. That's an extremely special clock indeed, I call it the 'Heart of Meridian', and it floats there because that's where it is now. It hasn't fallen yet, so it's still there. See? Time is all a matter of context when you think about it."

"Uh huh, right." Chase could see that there was a logic of *some sort* in there – s*omewhere*. "How is the place so big? It's way bigger than it should be. Wait, hang on – don't tell me, I'll guess – time-shifting Inca magic?"

"Close enough," replied Alejandra. "Time and space are pretty much the same thing, really, like plaits that are wrapped around each other, but all attached to the same head in the end. If you can bend one, you can bend the other."

Chase's eyes roamed around the extraordinary place she had brought him to, trying to take it all in. A series of doors ringed the circumference of the gigantic space, each one about four feet tall and arched, like a church door. Directly opposite where they had entered, a large stone archway led off into the unknown, a soupy grey mist hanging in the air beneath its mighty keystone. In the centre of the chamber, a shabby old chest sat beside a simple wooden writing desk on a threadbare rug. The homely scene appeared oddly out of place in a room so grand in scale. He pointed to the small, arched doors. "Where do they go?"

Alejandra's face fell; her whimsical manner vanished in an instant. "I'm sorry to show you this, but it's best you know." She pulled one of the doors open with a loud *creak*.

Chase stumbled backwards as his knees buckled and the air rushed from his lungs. Brightly coloured dots danced in his vision like when he stood up too quickly. "Who's that?" he gasped.

Behind the door sat a young man. He was only a year or two older than Chase, but his clothes were different, old-fashioned. The collar on his orange shirt was almost comically oversized, and the bottom of his cord trousers flared out. A beige kipper tie finished the look of someone who had last got dressed in the 1970s. The young man was sitting bolt upright and totally still, his eyes were glazed over, and he clutched a fountain pen tightly in one hand. "What's wrong with him?" asked Chase. "Is, is he... dead?"

"No," Alejandra sighed and closed the door. "He's alive, but time-locked. He's still living in a single second that for the rest of us passed by in the blink of an eye, more than 40 years ago."

"Did you do this?" Chase started slowly backing away from her, preparing to make a dash for the stairs. "Do all these doors have someone trapped in time behind them?"

"No, I didn't and yes, I'm afraid they do," she replied. "I

call them my 'forever people'. This is Van-Quish's doing, not mine – he trapped them like this."

A *whooshing* sound roared in Chase's ears, sweat beaded on his forehead and he felt an urgent desire to throw up. "Can't you help them?" he croaked.

"Technically... yes. *If* I had the complete, undamaged Time Driver, it might be possible to return them to our time stream. But even if, by some miracle, their bodies survived the sudden surge forward in time – which most of them wouldn't – can you imagine what it would do to their minds? Some of these people have been down here for hundreds of years now, everything and everyone they knew is long gone. All I can do for them is to keep them safe and alive – in a sense. As far as each of them is aware, they still exist in a single instant of their lives. They just don't know that that single instant is now their forever. Like I said before, time is all about context."

"But who *are* they?" asked Chase.

"You wanted to know what I meant earlier when I said 'we' tried to stop him. Well, some of these are the 'we' I was talking about. People who happened across me and wanted to help. Others are poor innocent souls who fell afoul of Thorne, or Van-Quish, or Bingham, or whichever of his aliases he was going by then. Everyone here, for one reason or another, ended up on the wrong side of the Time Driver. This is Fernando's way of punishing those he feels have wronged him. So, whenever I could, I brought his victims here for safety, and to spare their families from seeing them like this. They would only think they could save them and waste their own lives trying. I know, I've seen it first-hand."

"Alejandra, how did Thorne end up running a school in Bisby? I mean, what's the point?" Chase asked quietly, as she closed the door on the poor time-locked man.

She wandered over to her desk and fiddled with a pile of papers there, gathering her thoughts. "It's quite simple, and also quite brilliant," she announced eventually. "Fernando's been experimenting with business for decades. He's used the Time Driver on his workforces innumerable times over the years and managed to amass an impressive fortune. Luckily, though, thanks to the ravages of time, and his ever-changing personalities, as far as I can tell, he's either lost his entire fortune, can't remember how to access it, or can't even remember having it in the first place. I haven't established yet whether his money is all sitting unclaimed in a bank somewhere, or if he went ahead and buried it all again..."

"Hang on," Chase interjected. "Buried it? Like buried treasure?"

"Of course," she deadpanned. "He's still a pirate underneath, after all. They don't change much, even after hundreds of years. Trust me on that!"

Chase shrugged his shoulders – there was that *"sort of makes sense"* again. She was good at that. "I see, but that doesn't answer my question – why's he in a school?"

"Well," she continued. "You see, Chase, the world changed more in the last 30 or so years than it did in the previous 300! Suddenly, it wasn't so easy to mess with time and not have adults notice that they'd worked 16 hours instead of eight. People nowadays have fancy watches and all kinds of technology. They have places to be and things to do. People understand time now, they see time travel on TV every day. The world these days is filled with complicated things that make life difficult for a hundreds-of-years-old-time-meddling pirate whose brain has been scrambled like an egg. But taking over a secondary school makes perfect sense because teenagers – no offence – are stupid."

"Wow... really? No offence?" retorted Chase. "That was actually pretty offensive!"

Alejandra placed her hands on her hips and pursed her lips, "Right now, you're what, 13 years old? And you've willingly gone into the locked basement of a disappearing magic shop with a *total stranger* who randomly gave you a gift and then showed you her very sharp sword, *and* the frozen people she has locked in said basement... And you say you're *not* stupid!"

"Well, when you put it like that..." Chase shuffled his feet awkwardly. He had to admit she had a point; he truly had been colossally stupid.

She grinned at him. "Like I said, teenagers are stupid! But if it's any consolation, they've *always* been stupid. It was the same in my day and that was a long time ago. I mean, I left my family for a backstabbing pirate when I was a teenager, so I can't talk! The thing about teenagers, is that as well as being stupid, they have zero idea of timekeeping, and zero common sense. They sleep at strange hours and wake at strange hours and have no clue about the big wide world, despite weirdly believing that they know *everything* about it! To the point where adults – who *actually do* know about the big wide world – get so tired of listening to them that..."

"That they don't listen to them at all!" finished Chase. "I see your point – if I was to tell my dad or Max or the police, or *anyone,* that my headmaster was a hundreds-of-years-old pirate, who was making lessons super-long and break times super-short by controlling time with a stolen Inca time-thingy that was a gift from a god, I'd... well, I'd be locked away! No one would ever believe me."

"Right," Alejandra beamed. "But that's just a handy side-effect. The government is offering a huge cash prize as an incentive to the best headmaster this year, and I think that's what Thorne has his eye on. It's something like a million pounds, I'm betting that my Fernando is buried deep in there somewhere whispering in Thorne's ear that he needs that money, and he probably has enough loyal friends in high places to swing it for him, too. In this world, getting his hands on that much wealth and influence could open a lot of doors for him that we *do not* want him to open. Can you imagine what could happen if he got into government!"

"This is making my head hurt," complained Chase. "Thorne is Van-Quish, but doesn't always *know* that he is?"

"Correct! Well done for keeping up finally," said Alejandra. "His brain has been scrambled by the effects of the Time Driver, but he's always the same self-serving old Fernando underneath. But there's more – think about it, Chase. Young people who've been brainwashed and educated by Thorne will grow up to become leaders and business owners and politicians..."

"...All unquestioningly loyal to Thorne with no idea why!" Chase concluded. "That has the potential to be bad, extremely bad – and he lives so long that he can afford to play as long a game as he needs to! Can you imagine a future with him pulling the strings? I've already had a taste of it, with his endless boring lessons and his insane rules. And he had his student reps try to beat me up."

The memory of his dramatic escape brought Chase crashing back to reality. "Oh man, I've got to go," he moaned. "I'm in so much trouble right now, I don't even know what to do. I set off the fire alarm and legged it from school. Thorne sent his goons to get me 'cause he saw me in some weird memory vision thing when I opened the watch. That's what I came here to ask you about in the first place!"

She turned on him, visibly shocked. "That's called a 'timestream'. When you opened the watch for the first time, yours and Fernando's streams must have somehow crossed for a moment. You say he saw you? Not good. Not good at all."

"Well, it's your fault that he's after me!" bleated Chase. "You gave me the watch! Wait... you gave... me... the... watch." His voice trailed off, he and Alejandra looked at each other for a moment. "*Why* did you give *me* that watch? Why me? Did you know this would happen? Is this how you got those 'for-ever-people' to help? Draw them in with free watches and weird visions and then..." A terrible thought occurred to him. "Is that how I'm gonna end up... stuck in one of your cupboards for all eternity?"

She made her way over to the impressive stone archway and entered the mists beneath, gesturing him to follow. "No, no harm will come to you, I promise. Look, before you go, let me show you something."

19

THE SEARCH

The early evening sky over Bisby glowed with vibrant hues of pink and blue, but Thorne's student reps were oblivious to the beauty above them as they gathered at the gate to the empty Connors house. Thorne had had them hunting for Chase all afternoon, but they'd found nothing. In a rage, he had dispatched the brainwashed teens to the Connors home with hockey sticks and instructions to enter by force and search the place for anything made of gold, any clocks or watches or anything resembling a crystal.

The reps didn't care how unusual the orders were, of course. Or that if caught breaking and entering that they would be arrested and receive a criminal record. They only knew that it was vitally important they follow their headmaster's wishes, no matter what. It never occurred to them to wonder why. The headmaster was not to be questioned – their loyalty to him was absolute.

It took only a few seconds for them to smash their way in through the kitchen window, and less than 15 minutes for them to ransack the house completely. Anything at all even slightly meeting Thorne's criteria went into the sports bag they had brought with them.

The reps were just in the process of making their escape when Max pulled into the driveway in his prized vintage car. "Hey, what the hell is this?" He opened the gull-wing doors and leapt from the driver's seat with his fists raised, leaving the lights on and the engine running. "Who are you?" he demanded. "What have you done?"

The student reps stared at him blankly, as he peered past them at the chaos beyond the wide-open front door to his home. "You've trashed my house you little..." A dreadful thought occurred to him. "Where are Jon and Chase? If you've hurt them, I'll..."

He never got to finish the sentence. Abigail Pansy bopped him straight on the head with an expensive-looking hockey stick, sending him slumping to the floor.

20

CONVERGENCE

"I followed Thorne, or Fernando Van-Quish as he was then, here to Bisby more than 250 years ago," explained Alejandra, waving away the grey mist that filled the archway.

She had led them to a small antechamber where a huge age-dulled mirror hung in an ornately carved frame of polished black stone. Flanking it were a pair of enormous hourglasses that were mounted to the wall through their throats. A tangle of thin golden vines emerged from the wall beside each hourglass and trailed along the dusty ground. Each 'vine' pulsated from within as though it were connected to a heart. Chase traced their path to a stone plinth in the centre of the chamber.

The top of the plinth was carved into an elaborate sundial, its pointed gnomon crafted from the same shiny black stone as the mirror frame and inlaid with fine gold filaments. A strong smell hung in the air, sweet and oaky with a hint of ozone. It reminded him of something, but he couldn't quite place it.

"Back in those days," continued Alejandra. "Van-Quish was being pursued by a particularly tenacious naval captain named James Harris – he's one of the forever people now, I'm sad to say. Anyway, Van-Quish's ship, *The Vehement Ranger*, had already taken several cannon hits and most of his brainwashed crew had perished. He lost control and the vessel was blown on to the rocks between Bisby and the Isle of Clod, near where the end of the old pier is today. Fernando chose to abandon ship and flee ashore to hide his precious treasure among the network of caves, chines and inlets that were here before the town was built. You mentioned earlier that you thought there was magic in Bisby, well you're right. Van-Quish had gathered magical artifacts from all over the globe for hundreds of years. Seven of them were hidden here in what is now Bisby. The Time Driver is one and I suspect your 'spinny thing' in the library is another."

"You're very good at not answering my questions," Chase noted. "This is a fascinating story, but it doesn't explain why you chose me, or what I saw in the watch."

Alejandra's face wrinkled and her shoulders stooped as age overcame her body once more. She lay a hand on his shoulder and looked him straight in the eye. "You're an auger, Chase."

"I'm a what now?"

Before she could reply, the sands within the hourglasses emitted a powerful golden glow and they started spinning on their axes, creating two large balls of light that chased the mists away. The vines trailing along the floor lit up like Christmas decorations, sending a burst of brilliance up the plinth and into the sundial. "Watch!" called out Alejandra, grasping Chase by the shoulders, and gripping him tightly. "But stay silent, not a sound! Understand?"

He nodded, despite not understanding at all, it was fear that was keeping him silent, nothing more. The atmosphere around them sizzled and crackled as if something was trying to rend the air itself apart. A sharp stench of ozone seared Chase's nose with each breath, and every hair on his body stood on end.

For a split second, he felt as if he was standing inside a light-ning bolt, being boiled alive. Then, a glaring beam of searing light tore out of the gnomon on top of the sundial, lanced across the antechamber and pierced the huge mirror.

The crackling stopped, and the air was still again. Every-thing was as it had been moments earlier – only now the surface of the mirror was no longer dull and worn, but gently rippling like a pond into which someone had tossed a pebble.

"Look inside," whispered Alejandra. "Look into the mirror and tell me what you see."

Chase peered into the rippling – what? *Glass?* No – what-ever was filling the inky black frame was no longer glass. It wasn't even solid. It was more like a faint liquid-silver veil hanging in mid-air. At first, he thought there was nothing to see but his own reflection, but the more he stared into the rippling silver curtain, the more he realised that the eyes looking back weren't his own. Something else was staring back at him, some-thing else with keen yellow eyes. More details started to resolve themselves in the darkness beyond the veil and he abruptly recoiled with ice in his veins. "I know this mirror! It was in the vision! And I know that place in there – it's the weird little study at school, the one with the owl in! Wait a minute – that leads to Thorne's office!"

Chase's heart slammed up into his throat and his knees turned to spaghetti as adrenalin flooded his body. "That owl led me *here*! You *are* in on this!"

Alejandra leapt for Chase as her body transformed once more, making her suddenly young again. She clamped a strong hand over his mouth and pulled him close. "Sssh! I'm not '*in on this*'. How do you think you escaped from Thorne's office and wound up on that bench?"

"Mumph mumph mumph?" Chase wriggled and raised an eyebrow.

"Yes, that was me. Now, if I let you go, do you promise not to freak out?"

"Mumph, mumph mumph."

"Good. I'm letting go now but keep it down, OK?"

She released her grip and Chase pointed to the mirror, then to Alejandra and then to the mirror again, his mouth agape.

"Are you seriously telling me that we're this close to the school?" he whispered. "What is this place? A spaceship or something? Have we tunnelled underground? And what's an auger? You called me an auger before."

Alejandra rolled her eyes. "I'm obviously not an alien – do I look like the spaceship type?"

"I dunno," replied Chase. "You have time-crystals and a disappearing shop, I mean – I have questions y'know! Lots of questions! And didn't Incas have giant metal Condors to fly around in, aren't those famous Inca lines in the desert to do with aliens?"

Alejandra's eyes bulged and her cheeks turned red. For a moment, she almost forgot to whisper. "What is it with you and aliens? Firstly, Meridian isn't a spaceship, it's a shop – sort of! It's a pocket, a great big time-pocket created by the heart of Meridian. And it doesn't *disappear* – it *hides* in time. Meridian is one big timey-hidey hole, time-slipping backwards and forwards, constantly moving. That's why you can't see it unless you have the watch – or unless it wants you to. Meridian is very old, you see, and with age comes quirks – this place has developed a bit of a personality of its own over the years. Meridian is what keeps me from aging too far and shields me from Van-Quish and the Time Driver. So, you see, Meridian is always *there* – it's just not always there *then*. And as for metal condors – *no*! Incas did *not* fly about in giant metal birds – where would you even get that idea? And those lines you're talking about weren't anything to do with aliens, they're called the Nazca lines and... well... that's a long story! We'd drunk a lot of wine and it seemed funny at the... look, we're getting off track. Focus, will you!"

She gestured at the shimmering portal, clearly keen to change the subject. "Think of this as a sort of time-bridge. I call it a *'convergence'*, a fissure in the fabric of time caused by the separated parts of the Time Driver crystal trying to reunite themselves. When a convergence opens, it tends to muddle times and places together, just like our own memories do – time's quite old, you know, it has a lot to remember. The convergence can only open in a straight line along the Time Driver's lifespan, so it always leads to places or times that the Time Driver existed within. In fact, think of it as less of a bridge and more of an echo in time. Sometimes it's *now* inside the convergence and sometimes it's *then* and sometimes it's both. For some reason, since Van-Quish became Thorne and took over that school, Meridian has been opening the convergence more often. It seems to have taken a liking for this same mish-mash combination of Thorne's office now and the lower decks of Van-Quish's ship, The Vehement Ranger, back at some point before it sank. It's smushed the two places and times together, putting the ship right over the top of the head's study. You've seen it – the place you wandered into when I rescued you. It sounds crazy, but... I think Meridian is using the convergence to look for you."

Chase peered into the rippling veil in the mirror frame, trying to absorb what she had told him, "So, you're telling me when I was in detention and I went in that creepy study, I was on a real-life pirate ship? In the past? I mean, it seemed weird at the time, but I didn't get a chance to think about it too much, *because someone knocked me out and kidnapped me!*"

"Keep it down, you don't want anyone in there to hear our voices, it could alert them to the convergence." She held a finger to her lips. As she did so, even more years slipped away from her. Chase had never seen her so young; she now appeared only a few years older than him. "I didn't *knock* you out – *you* fainted from hanging around in smushed-together space-in-between-space-and-time for too long while you were bleating about a plaster like a big wet blanket. And I didn't 'kidnap' you, either – I rescued you! *And* I tidied up your mess and finished your lines for you, so stop moaning! And anyway, if anything, you should blame Argus for bringing you here."

He stared blankly. "You still haven't told me why or how Meridian is looking for me *or* what an auger is and now there's an Argus too! Who the heck is Argus?"

"You know Argus, you've met him," replied Alejandra. "Argus – the owl – he's a verger."

Chase's temples throbbed and it felt like his brain was about to trickle out of his nostrils. "So let me get this straight," he sighed. "My headmaster is an ancient immortal pirate who stole a gift from the gods called a Time Driver. You're his Incan ex-missus, who lives in a sentient time-slipping shop with a time-bridge in the cellar, along with all your frozen old mates, only the bridge isn't a bridge. It's a confused echo called a convergence that appears inside a mirror hooked up to a sundial and some hourglasses. And on top of all that, I'm an *auger* – whatever that is, and there's an owl named Argus but he's not just an owl, he's a 'verger'. Am I right?"

Alejandra seemed pleased. "Yes, correct! Well done for keeping up! See, I knew you were special!"

Gritting his teeth and trying his hardest not to throw his hands up and walk away, Chase forced himself to sound as polite as possible, "Alejandra, I know you've been alone for a really long time. But please – for goodness' sake, *please* – could you imagine for a minute that I have never heard of an auger, or a verger or any of this weird stuff and," he went on, raising his voice to his most shouty whisper: "EXPLAIN WHAT THE HELL IS GOING ON! PLEASE! In a super-simple way?"

She pondered this for a moment and then replied: "It *is* simple, dummy. Augers are rare people who are born with the ability to see through time. Augers get something like déjà-vu, but instead of seeing things they've done, they see things they're going to do. 'Future déjà-vu' if you like. Vergers are time-guardians, well, more like time-caretakers, really. They keep time neat and tidy and watch out for anything making a mess. Argus is particularly good at it; we've become quite close over the years he and I, what with all our chasing around clearing up after Fernando. The other vergers don't like me very much, they think I shouldn't exist here in this time, and that I'm too messy. They blame me for Fernando's antics and won't listen to a word I say. But Argus is different, much less grumpy than the others – he put me on to you, as it happens. He spotted you right away, took quite a liking to you – it's been an age since we found an auger like you."

"What do you mean '*like me*'?" asked Chase.

"You're an auger who's a natural-born rule-breaker, Chase – the perfect combination for stopping Van-Quish! Most people don't think about time, it's just numbers on a clock and whether they're early or late for something. But you – you *do* think about it, am I right?"

He shrugged his shoulders. "Since I was a kid, I never really thought about why – everyone has a thing, some people love books or make-up or whatever – I love watches and clocks and time – it intrigues me. Time's my *thing*, I guess."

"And now you know why – you were born an auger. One of life's many little mysteries." She waved her hands in the air as if drawing back a curtain. "Augers see time as more than numbers; they can see what has already been and sometimes even what's still to come. It's all time – it's always *there*, it's just not always *now*! Like a mountain, that's always there and is always taking up a load of space, even if no one's looking at it – time's the same."

"Actually," grinned Chase. "That almost made sense, but why is Argus an owl?"

"Simple," replied Alejandra, her hair turning darker and her face growing even younger. "Because time is big and complicated and old – and owls are wise and old. You've heard of 'wise old owls', right? Well, the *reason* they're wise and old is because they're the caretakers of time. They potter about, keeping an eye on big things with their big eyes and fixing stuff when they can. That's what caretakers do."

"What?" Chase roared. "That makes no sense whatsoever! And by the way, you've turned really young now. I don't want to be rude, but, what if you turn into a baby, or a pile of dust and bones?"

She rolled her eyes for the third time in as many minutes. "I've been time slipping between old and young for hundreds of years and it hasn't happened yet." She held up her newly young hands and examined them. "To be honest, though, once I ended up so short that I couldn't reach the... Hey! Come back!"

While Alejandra was distracted by staring at her own hands, Chase took the opportunity to leap through the convergence. She lunged after him but tripped over the tangle of golden threads connecting the hourglasses to the sundial plinth and crashed to the floor in a heap. "Stop!" she tried to whisper-shout. "You can't go charging in there! We need to plan, to think ahead, what if he's there and you suddenly appear out of nowhere! You'll ruin everything! Argus, stop him, please!"

The urgency in her voice only spurred Chase on. "Enough talking, you wanted a rule-breaker, and you got one!" he hissed back at her through the veil. "I've had enough of all this craziness! I want to see what's in there and I don't care what you say!"

Then, fuelled by the obstinate rebellion of youth – and more than a little anger at Thorne, he charged past the owl, through the section of the Vehement Ranger that he had seen before when it had replaced the study, and flung open the door to Thorne's office...

Only it wasn't.

Instead of the modern office with its weird wall of white clocks, he found himself in an old-fashioned ship's cabin.

Where Thorne's desk should have been, there was now a large table strewn with maps and charts, one of them impaled by a dagger with a golden blade. A luxurious four-poster bed dominated the room and, instead of beige blinds looking out over a car park, the window was completely transformed into a multitude of square panes, lashed by the grey sea beyond. The wall of blank clocks was gone and, in their place, stood a grand fireplace where a familiar object took pride of place on the mantelpiece: A red crystal shaped like an hourglass, but chipped and damaged, sat within a golden frame, gripped tightly in place by a pair of decorative armoured gauntlets protruding from the wall. "The Time Driver!" gasped Chase. "I'm on the Vehement Ranger again!"

As he spoke, the pocket watch, long-since forgotten, pulsed against his leg like a heartbeat. He pulled it out and turned it over, being careful to avoid the latch. The fine lines covering its surface had begun to glow and the faint pulse he had sensed before was much stronger.

He took a step towards the Time Driver and a searing pain sliced through his stomach causing him to bend double in agony. Around him, the air shimmered and filled with faraway voices.

"We searched... house, he wasn't... all we found." A muffled bang gave Chase a jump.

"Get on... keep look..."

The disembodied voices sounded closer, but still subdued, as though heard from another room.

"...Decide what to do with these two."

A sudden chill descended over the cabin. Chase's eyes grew wide as his breath condensed into a cloud of ice crystals that hung motionless in mid-air. For a moment he was entranced by the beautiful cloud. And then the ghosts came.

Milky-white figures faded into existence all around him. Featureless shadows, vague human forms in silhouette only, one tall, two short, and two indistinct blobs that were different from the others. He held his breath as the spectres moved around him, seemingly unaware of his presence as he slowly inched towards the fireplace.

He was just about to lay his hands on the Time Driver, when the air grew colder still, and the distant voices grew louder. The fireplace and the Time Driver sitting upon it faded away, replaced for a moment by a wall of featureless white clocks. Chase spun on the spot. The entire cabin was *dematerialising* – there was no other word for it! It was all still there, the table, the maps, the dagger – but Thorne's office was trying to force its way through. It was like being inside a badly tuned television, with the ghost of one channel appearing over the top of another.

"Oh no!" he whispered. "Not now! Time's un-smushing!"

The ghostly figures were becoming clearer by the second. Chase's blood ran cold. There was no mistaking them now – the ghosts were Thorne and his reps. They were *right there,* mere feet away from him but also *not quite there,* still mostly transparent, and out of focus. He pressed himself into the wall, praying that he was still invisible to them, knowing it was only a matter of time before the walls – or whatever time had for walls – separating the office in the present and the Vehement Ranger in the past broke down completely.

"Might... these two... like... for ever,"

There was no mistaking that voice, the tallest phantasm was Thorne, or Van-Quish or whatever his name was. That meant the others had to be reps, probably Pansy and Pritchard. The weird blob shapes remained a mystery, they were still more indistinct and not moving at all.

Holding his breath, Chase slowly crept back towards the entrance to the study, where he had entered through the convergence. The apparitions became more solid and more *real* with each passing second, and he was certain he was becoming more visible to them too. Ignoring the burning heat from the glowing pocket watch tightly clutched in his hand, he desperately fought down the urge to run and tried to keep as low and slow as he possibly could, hoping that time would stay on his side for once.

He was three steps away from the safety of the convergence when the two mysterious, unmoving blobs finally took on enough detail for him to make them out. What he saw stopped him in his tracks.

It was Delyth and his father.

Their translucent forms were clear enough that he could see they were both clutching something and squatting awkwardly, as if they had been sitting and had their chairs pulled out from under them but were yet to fall. They were frozen into a single instant, time-locked like the forever people back in the chamber. Fear turned to white-hot rage. Chase abandoned all thoughts of a stealthy escape and screamed at the top of his voice: "WHAT HAVE YOU DONE TO MY DAD?"

With a guttural scream, he hurled himself at the

Thorne/Van-Quish-shaped apparition, but before he could reach him, a woman's voice rang out: "NO!"

Then time and space broke.

The two overlapping places and times that the convergence was forcing together like a badly fitting jigsaw were torn apart by Chase's attempts to be in two different places and times at once. A jagged tear appeared out of nowhere, splitting open the fabric of time and space. A gaping wound that looked like a miniature black hole had been drawn from the depths of space and deposited between the two points that Chase was trying to occupy.

Alejandra's eyes widened as she emerged from the convergence. "Chase, look out, it's a time-rip! Argus, help him, please!"

On one side of the time-rip, Chase Connors launched himself off the deck of a long-sunken pirate ship, intent on hurling himself across the void to exact revenge on the headmaster from hell.

Time slowed to a crawl.

On the other side of the rip, the shell of a man that was headmaster Angus Thorne closed his eyes for the last time and fell away into darkness, yanked back into the labyrinth of his own convoluted mind by the fearsome force of will that was his true self – Captain Fernando Víbora Van-Quish. His body twitched and jerked as the pirate's ancient, time-addled brain adjusted itself back into his familiar old body and his memories flooded back. "My ship!" he roared. "What are you doing on my ship?"

"Argus, now!"

A huge black shape filled the air like a demon from the

underworld. It swept past Chase blocking his path and stopping him in his tracks on the ship side of the time rip.

Argus, the tatty old owl that had first drawn him into Meridian, didn't seem so tatty anymore as he extended his powerful wings and unsheathed his deadly talons. The verger hurled himself at Van-Quish and the reps over and over, beating them with his wings, slashing at their arms and pecking at their faces.

"Run!"

A pair of hands yanked Chase back into the convergence. He stumbled through the door, through the mirror frame and back into the antechamber beyond where Alejandra threw herself to the ground and grabbed a handful of the golden vines running to the sundial. She hesitated for a moment, looking back over her shoulder. "Come on Argus, come on." A second passed, then three more. One went away, then another two came. Time ran out.

A blood-curdling *shriek* echoed from the convergence and was suddenly cut short. Chase watched with bated breath, but nothing else came through. With an anguished wail, Alejandra yanked the vines from the sundial.

Sparks lit up the antechamber and the air crackled as the gnomon's light flared for an instant.

Then the convergence was just a dusty old mirror again.

Across town at the academy, the office was just an office.

And deep below the waters off Bisby, the Vehement Ranger was nothing but a long-lost wreck, rotting on the seabed.

21

WHAT ONCE WAS LOST

F ernando Van-Quish glowered down at the lifeless owl lying at his feet, his newly restored mind racing to rebuild his splintered memories as it took its rightful place at the front of his time-fractured brain once more. *"That voice? It couldn't be."* Blood ran down his face and pooled on the pristine floor as he knelt to the examine the prone bird. "Argus?"

"Eeeew! Gross! Oh my God, there's a dead bird! What's happening?" Abigail Pansy was verging on hysterical, the spell that usually maintained her cold demeanour very much broken. Richard Pritchard, meanwhile, quietly sobbed and clutched at his swollen wrist.

"Sir," he blubbed. "Your eye! It... it's..." His voice trailed off as a wave of panic overwhelmed him. "What happened? Where am I?"

"OUT!" Van-Quish didn't need to tell them twice; a deathly pall fell over the pair as they slipped back under his thrall. "Find me a crew!" he barked. "I'll retrieve my ship – be ready to man the cannons!"

"Yes, Headmaster," they intoned, wandering off with their own injuries seemingly forgotten.

Van-Quish rose to his feet, his left eye dangling from its socket like a grisly yoyo. Without so much as a grunt, he casually popped the damaged orb back into place with a meaty *squelch* and rolled it around a few times. It remained grey and sightless, and an ugly gash bisected his face straight through the socket and down his cheek. Showing no sign of pain or emotion, he reached into his desk drawer and produced a small wooden box from which he retrieved a plain black eyepatch. "An eye for an eye, Connors," he growled.

"Now what about you, Verger?" He examined the motionless owl and looked around his office suspiciously. "Where could you have possibly come from?" His eyes fell on the glow being emitted from underneath the wall of clocks. "Or should I say *when?*"

22

EVERYTHING IS STUPID

Alejandra was furious, her cheeks had turned a deep violet and the finger she was aiming at Chase's face was visibly trembling. "Why would you do something so stupid?" she demanded.

"*You're* the one who said teenagers are stupid!" he fired back. "I'm a rule-breaking teenager, remember! That's what you wanted, isn't it? Well, that's what you got. Maybe *you're* stupid for wanting me! This shop is stupid and this whole 'Time Driver' thing is stupid, too! In fact, you know what? *Everything* is stupid, and I've had enough!"

They glared at each other in a sullen silence, the air around them fraught with tension and heavy with the reek of ozone given off by the convergence closing. "I'm going home," announced Chase. "I need to check on Max and go rescue my dad and Delyth from your crazy ex-boyfriend's time-lock. You stay here and hide – that seems to be what you do best anyway." He stomped off back through the main chamber, past the doors housing the forever people, and made his way back up the stairs through the clock to the shop.

"Chase, wait," Alejandra called out as the front door slammed shut.

Once he was outside, Chase flipped open the pocket watch and read the inscription once more. Then, with a sigh, he latched it shut and Meridian vanished from sight.

Max was still in the driveway when Chase arrived home. He had pulled himself into the seat of his car and was yelling into his mobile phone while dabbing a handkerchief on his bloodied head. "I don't care what situation he's dealing with! You tell that headmaster that some of his pupils assaulted me and ransacked my home! In full uniform! I'm coming to the academy now and I want answers, and you better believe I'm calling the police to meet me there. I don't care how busy he is, tell that headmaster he'd bett..." The sight of Chase charging up the driveway, visibly distraught, stopped Max in his tracks. "I've got to go, but this isn't over." He hung up the phone as Chase leapt into the passenger seat and threw his arms around him.

"Max," he sobbed. "Are you OK? What's happened?"

"We've had a break in – it was some kids from that academy of yours. I've been assaulted but I'm not worried about me. What's wrong with you? You look terrible."

"Drive me to the school, please – Dad's in trouble. Thorne's got him, I mean Van-Quish, I mean... It doesn't matter, Dad's trapped, we've got to be quick or... Look, I'll explain on the way." He paused. "Not that you'll believe me."

Max broke free of Chase's embrace, "Hey, calm down, you're not making any sense. Who the hell is Van-Quish? What do you mean Jon's in trouble? What's going on here?"

Chase didn't bother to answer, instead he reached over,

twisted the ignition key, and released the handbrake. Then, ignoring Max's protestations, he yanked the gear stick into reverse and shoved Max's foot down hard on the accelerator, sending them hurtling backwards down the driveway in a shower of sparks. Both the car's gull wing doors slammed shut with a loud *bang*. "I said DRIVE!" he yelled. "NOW!"

Across town in the Academy for Raising Standards in Exceptionalism, Fernando Van-Quish turned to the wall of clocks in his office and slid open the blank panels beneath them in sequence. Behind each panel lay a keypad, into which he typed a different sentence:

"The moment we met."
    "The first time she said: 'I love you.'"
    "The hour she betrayed me."

For each sentence he typed, the hands on the corresponding clock spun around to mark a different time. Once every clock had moved to a new position, a muted *thud* reverberated through the floor and a seam of light appeared in the wall. A golden glow flooded the room as the wall slid back to reveal a vast nothingness beyond.

Van-Quish stared off into the impossible void, a sneer etched on his disfigured face. "Now," he growled, "to business."

He strode into the abyss and the wall closed behind him, stranding him alone in a featureless white landscape stretching out into infinity. Discarded trinkets from every corner of the globe lay haphazardly strewn about here and there, the detritus of hundreds of lifetimes, relics of his many long-forgotten identities. As he walked, time lost its grip on him, as it had with Alejandra in Meridian. For an instant he was withered and old, but then youth reclaimed him, and he marched onwards with the vigour of a man in his 20s. Seconds later, coarse bristles sprouted from his chin and grew into a long, dark beard with twin streaks of grey running down its centre like fangs. Creases formed around his eyes and locks of greasy black hair descended his shoulders and ran down his back. Time seemed to like this version of him, for that is where he stayed.

Despite there being no kinds of landmarks at all, not even a horizon, the transformed Van-Quish knew exactly where he was going, turning this way and that until finally, he ground to a halt in front of a tatty old wardrobe standing alone in the empty landscape.

He studied it for a moment, gently caressing its crazed lacquer as if it was the cheek of a long-lost love. Then he reached into his shirt, still spattered with the blood he had spilt as headmaster Thorne, and withdrew a silver necklace bearing two small keys, one black and one gold. He thrust the black key into the wardrobe's lock and fumbled for a moment before triumphantly yanking the doors open.

A long, black coat and weathered hat hung inside, both decorated with a 'skull and swords' motif carved from blackened human bone. A thick bandolier hung beside a Japanese sword and a gun belt containing a pearl-handled pistol.

At the base of the wardrobe was a simple trunk, which Van-Quish unlocked with the second key. He carefully lifted open the lid and gazed down at the contents as golden light washed over him from within. Nestled in its frame at the bottom of the trunk, was a crystal shaped like an hourglass, chipped and incomplete, stained red with blood... The Time Driver.

23

THERE'S NO SUCH THING AS

"Look out!" shouted Chase as Max threw his car around a particularly tight corner.

"I wouldn't *have* to look out if you'd stop babbling gibberish about time-travelling pirates – it's putting me off!" Max slammed the car into second gear and gunned the throttle, but not much happened. His retro sports car looked amazing with its stainless-steel body and gull-wing doors, but the engine didn't live up to the sporty promise of the outside. "I think you need help, Chase," he shouted over the screaming engine. "It's OK to ask for support, you know – all this blowing up school and detentions and acting out about time pirates. It's all a plea for attention. Being a teenager is tricky..." He slewed the unwieldy car around the bottom of the steep hill leading to the seafront in a cloud of tyre smoke. "Believe me, I know. I was young, too once, you know. I remember back in the... woah!" He slammed on the brakes, bringing them screeching to a halt. "What the hell is all this now?"

The entire promenade was at a standstill. Max raised the

doors, climbed out for a better look. He stepped into a cacophony of honking car horns and angry shouts. "We don't have time for this – what's going on?" seethed Chase, climbing out of the car after him. "I'm serious, Max, I know it sounds crazy, but dad is in real trou...What the..?"

A long procession of academy students was crossing the road ahead of them, making their way down to the promenade in complete silence, completely blocking the way forward. The teenagers moved like robots, marching one behind the other, shoving aside anyone who happened to be in their path as though they simply didn't exist. A young girl went flying and her father grabbed one of the students by the arm. "Hey, watch where you're going!" His wife shouted at him to stop, and he hesitated, torn between tending to his child and chasing down the culprit. "Freaks!" he bawled after them, scooping up his sobbing daughter.

"It's more nutcase kids from your school," said Max, concern etched on his face. "Do you know about this?"

"Kind of," said Chase grimly. "I think this is all my fault."

The students bashed and shoved their way through the thronging mass of tourists wandering around Bisby promenade. They marched as one, in total silence. Their faces were locked into a stony gaze, oblivious to the shouts and threats directed at them as they trampled anything and anyone in their way, even going so far as to clamber over the handful of cars that happened to block their path. An elderly gent in a luxury convertible had the shock of his life as dozens of teenagers simply walked straight through his car, trampling all over the leather seats and expensive paintwork while he cowered in the driver's seat.

Word soon spread, and a crowd gathered, many of them

wondering if it was all part of some protest or art performance. But curiosity gave way to fear and confusion as more and more people fell under the inexorable march of remorseless teens. A lone policewoman bravely faced down the silent mob with her baton, but she, too, was flattened under their feet.

A sobbing woman appeared from the crowd of onlookers and pleaded with one of the students, "Lucy it's me, Mum, what are you doing? You're hurting people. Stop, Lucy, please stop!" There was nothing – not a single flicker of recognition. The girl simply barged her mother aside and continued her march unabated, just missing a pushchair as she wandered on like a zombie.

"Hey you!" Max grabbed the nearest student by the sleeve. "What's wrong with you, man? You're hurting people, you nearly hurt that kid." The student didn't seem to see him and simply walked on, effortlessly tearing out of his blazer, leaving Max clutching the tattered remains.

"They're heading to the old pier!" shouted a voice in the crowd. "Look!"

Sure enough, the students had changed course at the unfinished Ferris wheel and were now marching towards the old Bisby pier. It had been boarded up a few years earlier after a mysterious fire had left it unsafe. Now it was little more than a rickety old walkway to nowhere. Since the new pier had opened, no one gave the old one a second thought, it was just another part of Bisby's strange and chequered history. Until now.

"Are you seeing this?" asked Max. "It looks like they're brainwashed or something. What's going on? And don't give me that garbage about pirates."

"I don't know what else to say," called Chase over the noise of the angry crowd. "I know it sounds crazy, but the headmaster's not who he says he is. He's hundreds of years old and he has powers, he..."

"WILL YOU SHUT UP!"

Chase was stunned. He had never heard Max raise his voice before – ever. But the man before him now was trembling with rage, his fists clenched and knuckles white. Dried blood still caked his forehead where the reps had attacked him. This was not the gentle and thoughtful man whom he had admired for so many years. "I told you," Max seethed between gritted teeth. "There's no such thing as time-traveling pirates, now we need to get to Jo..!"

An ear-splitting *crack* rang out over the town and the sun vanished, plunging them into darkness. Max and Chase wheezed as the air was sucked from their lungs and a powerful gale knocked them off their feet. As quickly as it had come, the dark was cast aside by a vast curtain of golden light that illuminated the sky, sending people scrabbling to shield their eyes from the sudden glare.

Out in Bisby Bay, the sea surged upwards with a tremendous roar, sending a huge wave tearing up the beach until it crashed over the seawall. Petrified screams rang out as the retreating waters dragged people and debris back towards the ocean's embrace. Everything and everyone that had been on the promenade moments earlier was now being smashed together in the raging torrent of receding seawater. People and pets fought to keep their heads above water as ice-cream stands, temporary tattoo stalls and all manner of seaside tat were sucked down the hill towards the sea.

Max threw himself at Chase and wrapped his arms around

him, clinging tightly to his precious car as the waters flowed around them. "Now what's happening?" he bellowed.

Chase raised a trembling finger to the sky. "That."

2 4

THE JUMP

An eerie silence fell over the town, broken only by the occasional sob and a deep rumble that came from everywhere at once.

The ghostly golden light faded, and the angry waves subsided as quickly as they had risen. The familiar glow of early-evening sunlight returned, bringing with it a sight the likes of which Bisby by the Sea had never seen before...

A colossal black hole had appeared in the air over Bisby Bay, barely 50 metres from the end of the old pier.

Max's mouth was opening and closing over and over like a dying goldfish as he gawked up at the roiling mass. "That," said Chase matter-of-factly, "is a time-rip. A really big time-rip. So do you believe me now?"

Max didn't answer, he simply slumped to the floor, unable to tear his gaze away from the chilling sight.

One by one, the town found its voice. Some screamed and some cried. Some prayed and others laughed hysterically. But the better part of human nature took over and tourists and locals alike banded together to help those who had been hurt in the chaos. "Hey," someone called out. "Those weird kids – they're not stopping – look!"

Chase looked at where the man was pointing. Sure enough, the entranced academy students were back on the move, picking themselves up from where the wave had sent them flying and resuming their mindless march towards the old pier and the time-rip hovering beyond.

"Max, come on, get up, we need to go," Chase insisted, when suddenly the rumbling sound emanating from the time-rip intensified. A deafening *crack* rang out and the tang of ozone and sweet burning wood filled the air. Somehow, Chase knew precisely what was about to happen, "Oh no," he groaned. "He's here."

"Look!" screamed a voice in the crowd. "Something's coming out!"

The tip of a huge sword materialised in the darkness at the centre of the time-rip's seething maw. It hovered there for a moment and then lunged forwards, revealing its bearer – a grotesque skeletal figurehead carved in golden robes, its face twisted into a maniacal grin, framed by lank ropes forming tendrils of greasy black hair. A pair of tattered angel wings splayed out of its bony shoulders, before flowing into the hull of a gargantuan black pirate ship bristling with cannons.

BWAAARR!

A terrible noise echoed over Bisby like a thousand foghorns

sounding at once as the Vehement Ranger emerged from the time-rip. The enormous ship appeared as though it had been dragged straight up off the seabed. Limpets and barnacles clung to her pitch-black hull and her maroon sails hung in tatters and water and seaweed poured from every porthole, knothole and gun port as the mighty ship settled facing the old pier with an almighty *creak*.

Along the seafront, the dazed crowds gawped in disbelief for a moment and then burst into rapturous applause as a bearded figure appeared on the ship's deck with his arms aloft.

But it wasn't the bearded figure that had drawn Chase's attention – it was the two limp forms dangling from a spar at the top of the ship's mainmast. "NO!" he cried. "DAD, DELYTH!"

"Oh. My. God!" Max turned deathly pale and started to shake. "It's true, it's all true! He's got my Jon up there, and he's not moving!"

Chase scanned the crowd. The mood had shifted from one of fear to jubilation, "Oh no, they think it's a show!" His voice leapt up several semitones. "Max, they think it's all part of a show!"

The line of students had almost shoved and bullied their way to the old pier's blocked-off entrance when a realisation hit Chase like a cannonball – like the very real cannonballs that would soon be raining down on Bisby if Van-Quish was able to get his brainwashed crew aboard. That had to be where they were going – to man the ship's cannons! He squinted down at the crusty old pirate. He looked so different from when he had been Thorne, but it was him all right. Hairier and scarier, for sure – but definitely him. *'It must be the Time Driver causing time-slips, like the ones making Alejandra's age jump about,'* he pondered. *'He looks just like the painting in his office.'*

As if he had somehow heard Chase's thoughts, Van-Quish turned to check on his captives, revealing the Time Driver attached to his back by its frame like a bizarre metallic rucksack. Apparently satisfied his captives were secure, the pirate stormed up to the ship's forecastle where two large objects slowly rose from the deck.

One was a menacing three-barrelled cannon pointed directly at the town, but the other Chase couldn't quite make out. For a moment he thought that it was a telescope, until he realised that the peculiar device wasn't a straight tube, but rather a gigantic, curved horn that looked for all the world like an oversized mammoth tusk that had been flared out at the end like an old-fashioned gramophone. Its purpose quickly became apparent.

"AUGER!"

Van-Quish's voice boomed across the bay, amplified by the enormous horn. "Do you see this? Do you see my prizes?" He pointed his sword up at Delyth and Jon as they dangled, time-locked and helpless, oblivious to their plight. "Reveal yourself, Auger, come on, Connors! I'll make you a deal, join my new crew, and serve as my personal time-seer and I'll let your father and the girl go. Or don't and I'll *let them go... straight to Davey Jones's locker!*" He gave a malevolent laugh and the clueless crowd applauded. "And once they've joined the briny deep, I'll start flattening this town piece by piece, until the people of Bisby hand you over anyway. Your choice, boy!"

The crowd gave an "*Oohh,*" and muttered among themselves as they looked around, all wondering if an actor was about to step forwards from among them and call the pirate's bluff in the unexpected free show.

All but forgotten in the excitement of the pirate ship's appearance, the spellbound students had forced their way over the barrier and had managed to get almost halfway down the old pier - which meant they were almost halfway to getting their hands on the Ranger's arsenal of cannons. A heavy knot formed in Chase's stomach. If they got to those weapons, Van-Quish could order them to blast the unwitting crowd to bits – not to mention the rest of Bisby. But there was no way to stop them, there was no way he could get there fast enough, unless...

"Max?" Max was staring into space, gibbering something about his subconscious creating illusions. He wasn't going to be helping any time soon – which only left one other option.

Growing up in a seaside town like Bisby has many benefits, not least of which is the presence of several gaming arcades, which was something that Chase had always taken full advantage of. Mostly he had played the games that paid out tickets or gave him the opportunity to score prizes like the poor departed Robowatch. But he was also quite partial to the odd driving game now and then and liked to think he was pretty good at it. He looked down at Max – who was drooling and gibbering. Then he looked at Max's car. The gull-wing doors were open, the engine was running and, most importantly of all... it was an automatic. How hard could it be?

"Sorry Max, I need to borrow the car." Without waiting for an answer, Chase leapt into the driver's seat and yanked on the straps to close the doors. It took him a few seconds to tighten his seatbelt and move the seat far enough forwards that he could reach the pedals. Then he was ready to do the most dangerous and stupid thing he had ever done...

Which was quite impressive, given the amount of times he'd destroyed the science labs at school.

He checked the route ahead; the road was totally blocked

with people, but where he was going, he wouldn't need the road! Mainly because, thanks to the spectacle unfolding in the bay and the big wave created by the time-rip washing every-thing away, the pavement was mostly clear. All he had to do was stay way over to the right. Admittedly, it wasn't a perfect plan. In fact, it was a downright terrible plan, but time, as usual, was not on his side.

"What will it be, Auger?" Van-Quish's gloating voice carried over the town. "Time's almost up!"

Chase shoved the gear stick into drive and smashed his foot down on a pedal. "Oops!" The car jerked heavily and bounced on its suspension. He took his foot off the brake and brought it down hard again – this time on to the accelerator and the vintage car shot off down the street.

He swung the steering wheel to the right and mounted the pavement with an expensive-sounding crunch. "Oops, sorry, Max," he winced.

Holding his breath, he floored the throttle and prayed that no one would suddenly emerge from one of the shops lining the pavement. If anybody stepped out, they'd be squished, but he couldn't imagine anyone was still buying buckets and spades when there was a gigantic pirate ship and a socking great black hole outside.

The crowd flashed past, and the engine screamed as he hurtled towards the roundabout at the bottom of the hill that would take him to the pier. Out of the passenger window, he could make out the Vehement Ranger looming ominously in the bay. He hadn't realised pirate ships were so big! It was enor-mous, more like a modern ship, but he didn't dare sneak more than a quick glance because it turned out that driving wasn't actually that much like the arcades at all, and if he hit some-thing it would be game over for real.

The roundabout came up fast. He leant hard on the brakes and slammed the wheel to the left, willing the aged car to make the turn. He fought down the temptation to close his eyes as the tyres squealed and the rear of the car slid around for a second or two. Strongly considering a change of underwear, he gunned the motor once more and headed straight for the closed off area that would lead him to the old pier and the Vehement Ranger beyond.

Thwack! This time he did close his eyes as the wooden barrier smashed over the top of the car, leaving a large crack in the windscreen. This was it – the old pier where he had been supposed to meet Delyth, back before things had gone completely bonkers! An unpleasant thought slowly dawned on him – The old pier. The VERY OLD pier! *'The hundreds-of-years-old, extremely rickety, badly fire-damaged, falling-apart-and-already-had-a-hundred-brainwashed-teenagers-shuffling-along-its-weakened-and-rotting-old-planks-pier'*. And here he was bouncing along it in a 40-year-old car that weighed a ton! What could possibly go wrong?

Deciding not to think about the watery grave waiting for him several metres below, Chase instead decided to focus on the only-slightly-less-pleasant thought that it felt as if his teeth would vibrate out of his skull at any moment. Out of his right window, he could see the line of brainwashed students, totally unperturbed at the sight of an old sports car bouncing past them down the pier. Ahead of him, the Vehement Ranger was coming about, ready to take on its kidnapped crew and bring its cannons broadside on to the seafront.

Time stopped.

A vibrant image popped into Chase's mind, as though it was being watched on a TV screen with all the settings messed up. He saw a silver car, buried in the deck of a ship.

In a snap, time began to move again.

The end of the pier was coming up fast.

"Future déjà-vu." gasped Chase. "Creepy! Well at least I know what to do, then! Geronimo it is... I guess." He squeezed his eyes tight shut, planted his foot on the accelerator and shoved the shifter from the drive position straight into first gear.

Several things happened at once.

The poor car gave an almighty *screech* as its aging gearbox imploded and shredded itself...

... The result of which, was to jam the back wheels down into the rotting wood at the end of the pier at great speed...

Which, in turn, chewed out a large hole, leaving the nose of the car pointing up into the air as the tyres bit into the crumbling wood one last time...

This resulted in Max's precious car being propelled upwards into the sky at tremendous speed with Chase still clinging to the steering wheel with his eyes tight shut...

As the rear wheels took flight, the not-very-well-made gull-wing doors popped open, briefly giving the doomed car the appearance of an ungainly robot-seagull....

Until it arced gracelessly back down towards the deck of the Vehement Ranger more like a big, shiny, expensive missile!

The damage caused by Chase's spectacular take-off proved to be the final straw for the poor dilapidated old pier and its sea legs finally gave way. The entire structure – and the mob of brainwashed students marching along it – plunged into the frothing waters of Bisby Bay far below.

When Chase woke up, he was pleasantly surprised to find out that he wasn't dead. Or at least, not until Max caught up with him, anyway. He clambered out of the wrecked car, which was now buried up to its middle in the upper deck of Van-Quish's ship, making sad ticking noises with all its lights flashing. "Huh," he sniggered to himself. "I guess that's why they call them 'gull-wing' doors."

LOOK WHAT YOU'VE DONE TO MY SHIP

C hase was rather impressed with himself. He had driven – and jumped – a car, *and* not died doing it. *And* he had stopped the students from getting to the Vehement Ranger. He had *even* found time to make a funny quip afterwards. In fact, he was just thinking that his rescue attempt might work out all right after all when...

"LOOK WHAT YOU'VE DONE TO MY SHIP, YOU OBNOXIOUS LITTLE CRETIN!"

Captain Fernando Van-Quish glared down from the fore-castle, his one eye burning with rage as he pointed his sword at Chase. Only the faintest hint of a likeness remained to show that he had once been headmaster Thorne. "I SHOULD SLICE YOU FROM POOP DECK TO BOWSPRIT!" he roared, sending globs of spittle flying in all directions.

Chase had no idea what either of those things were, or if he even had them in the first place, but the thought of being sliced anywhere sounded painful and not like something he was up for. "Your ship looks rubbish anyway!" he hollered back. "I mean, look the state of it! If you could pull it out of time, why didn't you at least pull it from the ship... *showroom* or whatever, so it was nice and clean!" He scooped up a handful of seaweed from the deck. "It looks like you pulled it up from the sewers or something! Gross!"

Van-Quish looked startled at this, as though it was something he hadn't considered. "I like it this way," he snarled. "It looks...what was it you said again? Ah yes, '*bussin'*.'"

Chase opened and closed his mouth a few times, searching for a suitable retort, but when nothing came to him, he settled for: "You give me back my dad and Delyth... you...you great big..." his mind raced, trying to pick the most despicable insult he could dream up, but the shock of having an actual sword pointed at him by an actual pirate had turned his brain to mush, so he finished with: "You great big... um... ninny!"

The pirate threw back his head and laughed the most unfriendly and unfunny laugh that Chase had ever heard. He wasn't in the habit of being threatened by laughs, but this one had menace, real menace.

"Oh, Chase, my boy," laughed Van-Quish, making a show of casually swinging the barrels of the huge triple-barrelled cannon round to face the town. "I'll make this easy for you – but this is your last chance, mind. Join me and I'll release your father and Maddocks, they'll be all safe and sound and you'll be a hero."

"What do you mean *join you*? Like, be a pirate?" asked Chase, stalling for time, and regretting not working out more of a plan before jumping on to a ship alone with a madman – an *armed* madman.

Van-Quish slid his sword back into its sheath with a *snick* and unhooked the Time Driver from his back. He placed it on the floor between them, spread his arms wide and gave an insincere smile. "As my own personal auger," he said warmly. "Think about it, my boy, with your ability to see through time, my long life, and the Time Driver, we could achieve *anything*! You could find us the perfect places and times to change the course of human history. Imagine – no more war, no more suffering, everything according to my – I mean *our* – design! We would be gods, Chase! You and me. Our names would be revered by every mortal to walk this earth for generations to come! Forget Bisby, lad, forget this whole tacky little island. We'll have the whole world at our feet – for ever!" The pirate stared down at him with a quizzical expression, "I said, we'll have the... whole... world... at... our... Oh for goodness' sake, CONNORS! WAKE UP! ARE YOU LISTENING TO ME, BOY?"

Chase was staring off into space. Something Van-Quish had said reminded him of something – something that he had missed in all the chaos. Then the penny dropped...

"Wait! I've seen all this before! Back in the study, before I fainted and Alejandra kidnap... rescued me!" He looked around. There was blue sky above, a gaping black hole behind him, and he was standing on a ship being threatened with a sword – exactly like the vision he'd seen after being hit by the exploding watch parts. *'Wow,'* he thought. *'Maybe Alejandra's right and I really am an auger! Maybe I really can see through time! I'm totally doing the lottery as soon as I'm old enough!'*

Empowered by this revelation, Chase jabbed a finger up at Van-Quish and stuck out his chin, "I'll never join you, Mr Pirate-pants! *I'm* calling the shots here now! And you're going to listen to *me!*" He raised his hand and counted off on his fingers. "*Firstly,* I've got no idea how all this *auger* business works anyway, I don't have a clue how to control it, so the joke's on you! *Secondly,* thanks to your stupid Time Driver thingy, you owe me a new watch! In fact, more like 10 watches. You owe me 10 watches you stupid... Oh no!"

Van-Quish hummed a sea-shanty to himself as he reached into his long coat and pulled out a lighter, which he nonchalantly held under the fuse of the huge triple-barrelled cannon aimed straight at the town. "*You're* calling the shots now, are you?" He sneered, "Let's see about that shall we!"

Chase's bravado failed him as his cheeks turned red and his knees went floppy. Auger or not, he suddenly felt very out of his 13-and-a-bit-year-old depth. "And... and another thing," he stammered, starting to panic, and really *not* doing his best thinking, "The Time Driver doesn't even belong to you anyway, it belongs to... oops!"

Van-Quish froze on the spot. His face turned black as night. "What did you say?"

"Nothing," Chase whispered and swallowed nervously.

The old pirate's good eye locked on to Chase. "What. Did. You. Say?"

"Nothing."

Van-Quish lit the fuse. "Fine, have it your way."

"NO! WAIT!"

It was too late...

A skull-crushing *boom* knocked Chase to the ground. His ears rang and his eyeballs vibrated in their sockets like bouncy balls. A sonorous *whump* impacted against his ribcage, squeezing the air out of his lungs and a high-pitched whistling sound came from somewhere.

Rapturous applause and delighted squeals went up from the crowd on the seafront far below the Vehement Ranger.

Squeals that quickly turned to screams as a cannonball tore into the almost-finished Ferris wheel with a deafening *crash*. Metal and wood fractured and groaned as two of the carriages plunged to the ground and burst, sending a hail of splinters over the terrified crowd.

Chiiiinnng.

Cold steel pressed against Chase's neck.

"I'll ask one last time," growled Van-Quish. "What did you say?"

A chill ran down Chase's spine. The temperature plunged. His breath fogged in the evening air and the hairs on his arms rose to attention. A crackle of static made his skin tingle. Bright blue sparks danced along the pirate's blade. There was a strange scent like, burnt wood.

A voice came from nowhere.

"He said it doesn't belong to you!"

Van-Quish froze on the spot. "It can't be," he spluttered. "You? How?"

Seeing a chance to keep his head attached, Chase rolled to the side and scrambled backwards along the deck, trying to put as much distance between the pirate's blade and himself as possible. As soon as he was clear, he leapt to his feet and searched around for the source of the voice. It didn't take long to find.

Far above him, near the top of the Ranger's main mast, where Jon and Delyth were still dangling, frozen in time, a doorway had appeared out of nowhere. Even in the already ridiculous situation in which he had found himself, it still took several seconds for Chase to process what he was seeing. A simple wooden doorway floated in mid-air, silhouetted against the backdrop of the gigantic time-rip. A simple wooden doorway with a brass plaque that read *'Headmaster's study'* – and a very welcome sight clinging to the doorframe.

"Alejandra!" roared both Chase and Van-Quish at the same time.

"About time you showed up," Chase called up to her. "How did you get up there?"

"The convergence, of course," grinned Alejandra, unsheathing her magical blade. "It was aiming for the study again, but missed a bit is all... went a bit high! Pulled off course by that socking great time-rip, I expect. Look, never mind all that, take this... stand back!"

She threw her sword down and it landed beside Chase with a resounding *clang*. He swept it up and wielded it firmly in both hands just as Van-Quish recovered himself long enough to scoop the Time Driver up off the deck.

"Freeze!" Chase pointed the tip of the weapon at the pirate, who simply ignored him and placed the stolen Time Driver on to his back once more. "I said freeze!" insisted Chase.

Van-Quish bared his teeth in an evil smile that reminded Chase of a cartoon shark. "Or what?" he snarled....

The pair circled each other, both totally unaware that high above their heads, a long stick with a hook on the end had quietly emerged from the floating door. It gently wrapped around the rope holding Delyth and carefully drew her back through the convergence into the safety of Meridian.

"Or I'll use my auger powers and chop you up!" retorted Chase.

The pirate laughed and feinted a stab. "You *do* know that isn't how auger powers work? I've had hundreds of years' experience in sword-fighting, boy. How many times have you ever wielded a blade?"

"Once," gulped Chase. "Including this one."

. . .

Far above the feuding pair, the long-handled hook appeared again, and drew Chase's father through the door, safely into the convergence.

Oblivious to the fact that his captives were gone, Van-Quish snarled at Chase: "I'll tell you what, boy. You tell me what you know about Alejandra, and I *might* show mercy and finish you quickly." He lunged forwards and Chase scuttled several steps backwards, waving his sword around like a flyswatter. "Speak! Or I'll gut you like a fish, boy, auger or not. You're meddling with things you don't understand."

"You've got that right!" said Chase. "Honestly, I have no idea what's going on right now! But if you don't let my dad and Delyth go, then I'll..."

"*Cooee!*"

A sharp whistle from above made both Chase and Van-Quish stop and stare upwards.

"On that note," breezed Alejandra from her floating door-way. "I think you'll find that particular issue is quite under control!"

Van-Quish took one look at the empty ropes dangling from the mast and his jaw dropped like a stone. "WHERE ARE MY PRISONERS?" he roared. "YOU'VE TAKEN MY PRISON-ERS! ALEJANDRA, YOU... YOU..." His mouth opened and closed a few times as he struggled to find the words. "YOU LOOK SO BEAUTIFUL; I'VE MISSED YOU SO MUCH!"

"Awww! Thank you, my love," replied Alejandra, turning a deep shade of pink. "You don't look so bad yourself – *for a lying, thieving ratbag!*"

The old pirate closed his eyes and drew a long, slow breath. A single tear leaked out of his good eye and trickled off into his matted beard. "Let's talk, my love," he pleaded. "I can explain everything... Right after I've *chopped up this landlubber!*"

He turned and swiped at Chase, who immediately panicked and swung his own sword blindly. More by luck than fortune, the two blades met with a *clang* and threw up a shower of sparks. "Help! What should I do?" pleaded Chase, glancing up at Alejandra, who was much too high up to be any use. "I don't know how to sword fight! I'm only 13!"

Another blow came, and again he parried, his arms weakening under the withering power of the older man's attacks. "Please, Alejandra, help me! He's too strong!"

"Remember," she called out to him. "'When time is a sword, let this be your shield!' You're an auger – use the watch!"

"WHAT?" squeaked Chase, rolling aside and dodging another deadly swipe. "Are you nuts? How am I supposed to fight a sword with a *watch?*"

Alejandra didn't answer, she simply closed the door and the convergence vanished, taking her and the rescued prisoners along with it.

"WAIT! COME BACK!" bellowed both Chase and Van-Quish together.

Alone once more, the two foes faced each other down. The blinking lights of Max's car, still half-buried in the deck, glinted off their readied blades. Behind them, the vast time-rip rumbled in the late evening sky, churning, and crackling as it shredded the walls between everywhen and everywhere.

"Do you know how many augers I've killed over the centuries, boy?" sneered Van-Quish. "They're always the same

– sanctimonious, self-righteous fools. Although, granted, I've never met one as young as you." He reached to his back and unhooked the Time Driver, holding it out in both hands. "But that won't save you. Time's up for you, Connors, you've cost me dearly here today. But I'm sure razing this town to the ground will make me feel a little better. Would you like to watch it burn – for ever!"

The Time Driver pulsed. A wave of golden light burst from the crystal and engulfed Chase, wrapping itself around him in flowing vines of shifting sand. His blood froze in his veins and time slowed to a halt as the time-lock took hold.

Despair overwhelmed him as the horrifying reality of defeat crushed his spirit for ever...

But it wasn't for ever.

Because he was a horologist.

He was an auger.

He was a rule-breaker.

He could *see* the sands of time as they engulfed him – and a time-lock was just time running slowly... But it *was* still running... which meant that he could still *see* it.

Alejandra had been right all along – time really was all a matter of context. Like when you're watching an aeroplane in the distance while travelling in a car. The plane appears to be standing still, frozen in time, even though it's actually moving much faster than you. Or when the clocks change for the end of summertime and suddenly, you're repeating an hour you've lived through once already.

Chase closed his eyes and focussed on nothing but the shifting vines of sand that had trapped him in the moment. A moment that was *now*, but could just as easily be *then*, or both, if he chose to see it that way.

He thought of the Heart of Meridian, the giant clock that always floated and never fell because it simply wasn't time for it to fall yet.

He thought of the moment he had blown up the lab at school – a single instant in time, so infinitesimally small, when two chemicals had met and reacted. And yet, that moment was still happening, for it had brought him here, to this – the fallout from that one tiny instant rippling across time and space.

He thought of the stars in the night sky. How we look up to them now and see light from suns that lit worlds and lives that faded and died millennia ago. Living memories, moments lost and forgotten, trapped in the darkness, only to twinkle and die in an instant in the eyes of the beholder.

It is always *then* and always *now*. The future can be the past, if seen from far enough away.

Context...

The sands of time encircling him pulsed faster and faster as their timestreams aligned with his own. Until finally, the time-lock broke. The vines uncoiled and crumbled into tiny golden grains that drifted up into the maw of the time-rip still hovering above the Vehement Ranger.

Van-Quish, consumed with rage at Alejandra's betrayal, prepared to fire the cannon once more. He chuckled to himself, cruelly aiming it straight down at where people were frantically trying to help the RNLI to rescue all the bewildered academy students from the tangled wreckage of the collapsed pier.

Chase fished out the pocket watch and flicked the latch.

The casing sprang open with a soft *click,* but instead of stopping and revealing the plain old clock face, it carried on opening. The rules of space and time gave up and went home as the decorated casing grew wider and wider, growing and spiralling open like an iris. The minute and hour hands folded in on themselves and ratcheted together, forming a handle that Chase gripped for dear life as the watch kept unfolding, transforming, and expanding before his eyes. Until suddenly, it stopped and locked itself into its new form with a sharp *snikt.*

"A shield!" gasped Chase. "The watch is an actual shield! – Oooooooh! I get it now, *'When time is a sword, this will be your shield!'* – Cool!"

The inner surface of the shieldwatch shimmered and rippled, no longer solid, but a liquid silver veil that he could see straight through. *'It's like the mirror in the Convergence!'*

The image of Van-Quish in the shield turned and gaped at Chase, his face contorted with shock. With a *yelp,* Chase looked over the top of the shield, directly at Van-Quish – only to find him still aiming the cannon and cackling to himself. Confused, he investigated the shieldwatch again. This time, the image of Van-Quish was storming towards him in slow-motion, mouthing something and drawing his sword.

He looked up again to find that the pirate staring at him in shock having heard his sudden yelp – exactly as he had been in the shield image moments before. "The future!" Chase gasped. "The shield's showing me the future!" He looked over the top of the shield again, only to find that this time Van-Quish really was storming towards him and drawing his sword.

"HOW DID YOU BREAK THE TIME-LOCK?" bellowed the raging pirate.

Deciding not to look over the shield again, Chase threw it up in front of his face and watched as Van-Quish made a powerful overhead strike. Which struck nothing but air, because Chase had already seen it and had simply stepped aside.

Again, and again the pirate swung his blade, using all his centuries of swordplay skills and tricks. And again and again, the blows rained down on nothing at all, as Chase the Auger dodged and ducked and slid and leapt about him in a blur. "How are you doing this?" demanded Van-Quish. "Stand still so I can kill you, boy!"

Seeing his chance to put some distance between them, Chase swung on to the rigging and clambered up to the after-deck. He lowered the shieldwatch just in time to enjoy the sight of Van-Quish huffing and puffing and angrily waving his sword about at places where he had been several seconds ago. "This is brilliant!" he laughed. "Oi '*Captain can't hit anything*', I'm up here!"

The pirate stopped waving his sword about and glared up at Chase, breathing heavily. He clung to a nearby rope and made a show of catching his breath. "A fool's move, boy," he panted, with a sly smile. "Only a landlubber would think he can run from a captain on his own ship." With a sudden swipe, Van-Quish neatly cleaved the rope and rode it upwards as its trajectory took it shooting up to the afterdeck. He landed close enough to Chase to strike him in the temple with a sharp *whack* from the handle of his sword, knocking him to the floor and sending the shieldwatch tumbling down to the main deck below, where it landed on top of Max's car with a *clang* and folded itself back into a pocket watch. "You should never have lowered that shield, boy," gloated Van-Quish. "Now it's mine – or at least, it will be when I kill you!"

He raised his blade and plunged it down toward Chase's stomach... which had inexplicably started to hurt.

. . .

Time stood still again. Very still.

There was a boom. A very big boom.

"*Aaarrggh! My hand!*" Tendrils of ice crept up the handle of Van-Quish's sword as a burst of Golden light flooded the deck of the Vehement Ranger. The old pirate threw his hands up to shield his eyes from the brilliant glare and tossed the frozen blade aside, clutching at his ice-burnt hand. "What's happening?"

Chase stumbled to his feet and checked himself all over to make sure he wasn't dead, which somehow once again he wasn't.

The sky turned black, and a strange sound filled the air, a sound like nothing Chase had ever heard before. At first, he thought it was thunder, or maybe the people down on the seafront clapping, but it wasn't a *clap*, it was more of a... *flap*.

No, not *a* flap... it was *lots* of flaps – wings flapping.

A great many wings flapping.

A *great, great* many wings flapping!

"NO!" roared Van-Quish, panicking. "NOT THEM! NOT NOW! NO!"

Chase took several steps backwards and raised Alejandra's sword, ready to defend himself. Van-Quish had completely lost his mind and was screaming and waving his hands around above his head.

"GET AWAY! LEAVE ME BE!"

The sound grew even louder.

Keen yellow eyes pierced the darkness as the sky became a living mass of razor-sharp talons and beaks and powerful wings.

"THE VERGERS!" roared Van-Quish. "THEY'VE COME FOR ME!"

He grasped at the Time Driver and held it high above his head, but no light burst from within. "WORK!" he shrieked, frantically waving the ancient device around, his single eye growing wider as the reality of what was about to happen dawned on him. "WHY WON'T YOU WORK!"

Chase threw himself to the deck and flung his hands over his head as a colossal parliament of owls erupted from the time-rip, blotting out the sky. A hundred vergers appeared, then two hundred. Then a thousand and ten thousand more. Every verger from across time filled the sky. Swooping and darting and dashing and diving on the pirate as he screamed and wept and waved his arms. "I didn't mean to hurt Argus!" he wailed. "It was an accident! I'm sorry! I'll be good, I promise!"

A particularly large owl swooped down and attached its mighty claws to the Time Driver. It stayed there for a moment, beating Van-Quish about the head with its wings, and pecking at his face, before tearing the device out of his hands with an angry *screech*.

As soon as the device was gone, another owl darted down. This one dug its talons into the pirate's shoulder. "OW!" he screamed, swiping away at the bird, but another sank its talons into him, and then another and another. Soon Van-Quish was wriggling and writhing as at least 20 owls grabbed at him from every part of his body. There were owls pecking his hair, owls yanking at his beard, owls tugging at his long coat, and owls pulling on his boots. He was drawn into the air, still struggling, and kicking and screaming as the vergers carried him upwards and off towards the hungry mouth of the time-rip. "NO! NOT THE RIFT! ANYTHING BUT THAT! PLEEA..."

. . .

Chase watched aghast as the vergers streamed back into the black hole. One by one, by 10 by 1,000, the owls carrying Captain Fernando Víbora Van-Quish vanished into the time-rip. For a moment his frantic screams echoed across Bisby Bay, before fading away for ever, lost in the space between everywhere and everywhen.

RUN!

F inding himself alone on the deck of a pirate ship teetering on the edge of a black hole in time and space was not how Chase had expected to end the day. Part of him wondered if he should be celebrating in some way, but he didn't really feel like it. The whole experience had been terrifying, and he just wanted to go home. But what would be waiting for him there? His life as he'd known it was over. His dad and Delyth were still time-locked. Both his house and Max's beloved car were wrecked. He had no school to go back to, and on top of it all, his head was pounding from where Van-Quish had smacked him with his sword.

He was still wondering what to do next, when the Vehement Ranger gave a loud *creeeeak* and shuddered beneath his feet. Then, with an even louder *groooan*, the rear of the ship violently lurched upwards and the entire vessel slowly started to move backwards as the gaping time-rip sought to return the vessel to its own timestream.

"No! No, no, no!" He bolted down to the main deck, where

a horrible realisation dawned on him. *"How am I going to get off?"*

The ship heaved again and gathered pace. The entire stern section, where he had been standing mere seconds before, had already been consumed. Cold spray stung his eyes as the enormous forces emanating from the ravenous tear in reality whipped the sea into a frenzy, dashing any hopes of surviving a leap overboard. Freezing wave after freezing wave pummelled the ship, knocking Chase off his feet and sending him flying.

The midship section vanished next, and he half-ran-half-fell to the bow where he clung to the rails for dear life. Far below, he could make out flashing lights on the shore as the emergency services tried their best to help the townspeople. They were tantalisingly close but might as well have been a million miles away. It was over, he'd lost, the maw was only feet away from him now and he'd be joining Van-Quish in the rift between time and space any second. There was no more time and nowhere left to run, only the Vehement Ranger's skeletal figurehead remained clear of the endless void.

Chase climbed out on to the grotesque winged skeleton; his frozen fingers as white as bone as he inched his way out to the farthest point of its raised sword. A desperate sob escaped his lips as the cruel waves battered him and the relentless nothingness kept up its unyielding pursuit.

Then with a violent *hiss* and the stench of burning, the time-rip finally collapsed in on itself and vanished, taking the Vehement Ranger and all traces of Fernando Víbora Van-Quish with it.

Chase closed his eyes and leapt off into thin air.

.   .   .

Hundreds of years in the past, the defeated ship returned to its watery grave once more, exactly as it had always been...
Almost.

EPILOGUE

C hase's breath froze on his lips.

A hand reached out and grabbed him.

He opened his eyes.

The floating door was back! And there, bathed in light, stood the person he most wanted to see in the whole world. "Dad!" he sobbed. "How?"

"Let's get you inside first shall we." Jon Connors hauled his son back through the convergence and into the safety of the chamber below Meridian. The two of them embraced for what felt like for ever and not long enough, until Chase finally pulled away.

"How are you OK? I thought you were time-locked?"

"We were," smiled Delyth, coming in for a hug. "But apparently we hadn't been locked for long, so Alejandra was able to free us."

"What, but how?" Chase clutched at his throbbing temple. The wound from Van-Quish's sword was starting to feel like nothing, compared to how much trying to figure out what was happening was making his head hurt. "I'm so confused right now."

"Well, that's nothing new!" Alejandra appeared from the stone archway with the Time Driver tightly clutched under her arm and a huge smile across her face, which was now somewhere in her mid-30s. "I'm glad you're OK, Chase, thanks for not dying."

"H... h... how?" Chase threw his arms around her. "Tell me everything."

"Well, if I must," she sighed, feigning modesty. "It *was* rather brilliant – if I say so myself. Do you remember how the convergence kept muddling up the study at the academy and Fernando's cabin on the Vehement Ranger?"

"How could I forget?" groaned Chase.

"And you remember that the wreck of the Vehement Ranger from *our* time is still out there at the bottom of the bay?"

"I hadn't really thought about that," he admitted.

She winked at him, "The devils in the details, Chase. Like the fact that when I first opened the convergence and gave you the sword, the effects of that massive time-rip pulled the convergence off course and the doorway appeared higher than I was expecting. Which came in handy to rescue these two, I might add! Well, I figured that, if I opened the convergence again precisely as the version of the ship you were on was vanishing, that it would open to *our* version of the ship, the one that's deeper because it's sunk! So, the height distortion caused by the rip before it vanished would put us at about the right place to help you out, which it did! And just in time, too! See, I'm a genius!"

"I knew time had to be on my side eventually," grinned Chase. "Thank you for saving them, but what did you tell them? How come they know about, y'know – Meridian and time and you and stuff."

"Time moves differently here, remember, Chase? Once I'd calmed them down, which I'll admit did take a while..." She gave Jon a friendly pat on the arm, and he grinned sheepishly. "We had plenty of time to have a nice cup of tea while I explained everything and contacted the vergers' parliament."

"But I thought you said they don't like you and that only Argus would listen to you?" asked Chase.

Alejandra folded her arms. "Well, funny story... I wasn't the one who persuaded them."

"It was me," announced Delyth, looking pleased with herself. "Well, *mostly* me."

"You... you talked to owls – and they listened?" said Chase. "But how?"

"Simple," she pointed an accusatory finger at him. "*I* speak sense, and, unlike *you*, owls are sensible creatures! I explained that Thorne, sorry... *Van-Quish* was a vile bully, and that the world has more than enough bullies already. Then I politely told them that he was putting children in harm's way, and that although it might seem like a trifling matter of a time-misplaced pirate ship to them, the entire situation had the potential to turn into something that would create far more mess in the long run. That, and the fact that he'd hurt Argus, was enough to persuade them that enough was enough, so they finally decided to put a stop to his antics."

"Point taken about the bullying," said Chase, turning some-what pink. "Thanks for persuading them – you saved my life!

I'd better add that to the list of things to make up to you somehow." He turned to Alejandra. "What exactly happened to Van-Quish, where did they take him?"

"Well," she replied, "Fernando is trapped in the rift – the space between timestreams. And, seeing as he lives so long, he's going to have a very long time to think about what he's done." She triumphantly held up the Time Driver, "As for this, the Vergers were good enough to return it – it is technically mine, after all! I plan on keeping it safe inside the Heart of Meridian, just in case the shieldwatch ever turns up again and I manage to collect all three parts."

"Oh," Chase's face fell. "The watch! I'm sorry, I didn't think to save it."

"Don't worry." Alejandra smiled and wrapped an arm around his shoulder. "I'd rather lose the watch than lose another friend."

"But what about you?" asked Chase. "What will you do now? You've spent years watching Fernando, and now he's gone. You didn't get any sort of closure, he just got... *owlified* and that was that! What happens to you and Meridian now he's gone?"

Alejandra pondered this for a moment. "Time will tell, Chase Connors, time will tell."

EPI-EPILOGUE

It was a wet Wednesday afternoon when Chase finally found Bisby Library again. He'd looked for it several times, but somehow never been able to track it down. But today was the day, and there it was in all its spooky glory, with its lion statues and big wooden door.... Only it was firmly closed, and a simple sign hung from the doorknob...

LIBRARY CLOSED UNTIL FURTHER NOTICE.
PLEASE POST ALL RETURNS THROUGH THE
LETTERBOX.

"You too, huh?" said a voice.

Chase nearly jumped out of his skin. A dark-haired boy had somehow appeared from nowhere and was standing right beside him. "Sorry, didn't mean to make you jump. I'm Jake." The boy held out a hand. "Jake Starling."

A QUICK THANK-YOU

Hello dear reader!

Thank-you for reading my book. I do hope you enjoyed reading about Chase and Alejandra as much as I enjoyed writing about them. I chose to set the story in an imaginary town called Bisby by the Sea, because it's exactly the sort of place I would like to live one day.

I loved writing my previous book set in Bisby (Jake and the Nefarious Glub) so much, that it got me thinking about all the other strange and wonderful people that live there and what their stories might be. Even before I had finished writing *Jake*, I already had a list of new ideas. I knew that I wanted to tell more stories about the unusual goings on in Bisby by the Sea, and Chase's story was one of the first ideas that came to me.

It was only after writing this story, that I realised that I might just have created a link between my two series, the "Bisby" books and the "Gideon Rayne" books... what do you think?

Anyway, watch out for more books from me in the future!

And if you enjoyed this one, please do leave it a review. Your opinion is important to us, and it really helps me out as an author and might mean that more people get to explore the weird and wonderful world of Bisby by the Sea, or the scary place that is New Britain in the Gideon Rayne books.

Take care and have fun

GA Franks

ABOUT THE AUTHOR

 GA Franks has a lifelong love of stories and writing. He is especially fond of the action-packed comic books of his youth in the 1980s. Originally from Leicestershire, he now resides in the picturesque Cotswolds with his wife and young children and works in education, alongside playing bass and guitar in bands.

To learn more about G.A. Franks and discover more Next Chapter authors, visit our website at www.nextchapter.pub.

The Time Driver
ISBN: 978-4-82415-487-3

Published by
Next Chapter
2-5-6 SANNO
SANNO BRIDGE
143-0023 Ota-Ku, Tokyo
+818035793528

26th October 2022